About t

Born in Taiwan and raised in Sweden, Kent has lived in Edinburgh since 2014.

He could never have imagined when he was struck by inspiration in 2016 that eight years later he would have written 200,000 words and that his third novel *Starry, Starry Night* would now be published. The initial idea came to him watching the TV program *Long Lost Family*. This novel is close to his heart, with themes of mental health and finding peace with the past.

As a writer, his aim has always been to create characters that are relatable and hopefully you'll find them emotionally engaging. Before starting as a novelist, he had eleven articles on food published in an English magazine in Brussels – and that laid the foundation for his writing.

Starry, Starry Night is the last of a trilogy following *Letting Go* and *Entitled*. He awaits the next step on his creative path.

Starry, Starry Night

To Callum !

[signature]

Kent Hung

Starry, Starry Night

Vanguard Press

VANGUARD PAPERBACK

© Copyright 2025
Kent Hung

The right of Kent hung to be identified as author of
this work has been asserted by him in accordance with the
Copyright, Designs and Patents Act 1988.

A CIP catalogue record for this title is available from the British Library.

ISBN 978-1-83794-335-7

Vanguard Press is an imprint of
Pegasus Elliot Mackenzie Publishers Ltd.
www.pegasuspublishers.com

First Published in 2025

Vanguard Press
Sheraton House Castle Park
Cambridge England

Printed & Bound in Great Britain

Dedication

Special dedication to the late Mr and Mrs John Teevan. They welcomed me, as an exchange student attending Ewing High School, to their home in Trenton, New Jersey, 1982–1983.

Acknowledgements

I would like to express my gratitude to those whose paths have crossed with mine, and to all the positive, negative, joyful, loving, heart-breaking, enriching, disappointing encounters, all of which have helped me to evolve as a storyteller and as well as a writer.

Many thanks to those who provided input to this novel. Special acknowledgements are due to Greig and Guglielmo – your valuable input and your continuous encouragement have made writing this novel possible.

Prologue

In July 1939, Freya and her husband were delighted with the birth of their first child, a baby boy. But their joy was overshadowed by the German invasion of Poland that triggered the Second World War. In fact, the Jewish community in Germany and other parts of Europe had already experienced racial, religious and political persecution before the war started.

In the beginning of the thirties, life had changed drastically for the Jews living in Germany. The Nazi regime expelled them from all kinds of professions and commercial life. Then, after the Second World War began, conditions soon became even more ungodly and horrific for Jews like Freya and her husband; the German government imposed severe restrictions and more discriminatory legislation on them, including reduced food rations and a strict curfew as well as a ban from designated areas in many German cities.

At first Freya, her husband and their baby boy were forced out of their home and moved to live in the Judenhäuser (Jewish houses) along with other families in an area designated only for Jews. Not long after, the authorities began to round up families from the Judenhäuser. Freya and her husband were separated and sent to different concentration camps. Later Freya learnt that her husband had been deported to Auschwitz, where he was killed. He was put in a gas chamber with thousands of others when the Nazis decided on extermination. Most heartbreakingly, at one point her son was taken from her. Her motherly instincts told her she would never see him again. For some unknown reason, Freya and a few other camp inmates were spared. None of this made any sense to Freya, who didn't comprehend why her husband, child and other family members had been so cruelly killed and why she had somehow survived.

Sometime after 1945, following Freya's liberation by Allied soldiers, she sought an opportunity to leave Germany, a place which bore too many painful memories for her. She first went to London as a refugee for a short period of time and then was relocated to Edinburgh, where she subsequently met Steve Hughes. They both worked in the same factory. Despite their age gap and Freya's struggles with her mental health due to her past, they got married in 1959. It was a year after they first met, she was forty and he was twenty-six. From a practical point of view, marrying Steve would make her stay in Scotland less troublesome when dealing with the immigration authorities.

Even though Steve was one of the very few people Freya got along with and let in, their relationship was not without challenges. Ever since they'd started seeing each other Steve noticed Freya's unpredictable need for periodic isolation. From what he could fathom, although she had survived the war, the inhumane treatment during her imprisonment in the concentration camp, the death of her husband and that of their son all had a haunting effect on her emotional stability and her ability to cope with life. After they got married, Steve was confronted first-hand by this harsh reality and evidence of her struggles. She would often simply ask Steve to give her space or just not engage in their daily life. On many occasions, as she detached from the world, he saw her tightly holding a photo of her son alongside some artistic postcards of paintings staring at them for long periods. Adding to their stress, Freya would have nightmares and often woke up screaming and in a cold sweat. She would also provoke fights, accusing Steve of judging her or saying something she took as an insult or criticism. This behaviour made Steve feel like he was constantly living on the edge. He was extremely worried and nervous as he didn't know how to handle Freya's unpredictable and explosive mood swings. What troubled Steve the most was discovering that Freya secretly harmed herself by cutting her arms and legs with razor blades. Steve was horrified the first time he woke up to find the bed sheets covered in blood from Freya's cuts. She would scratch the wounds during the night while in a sleep state.

Despite all the hardships, Steve adored Freya. Steve found a maternal figure in her because she was older and he looked to her for a kind of motherly love he'd never received from his own mother. Freya became his only family and he hers. There were good moments too. When she was calm she was the sweetest person. She cared for

Steve, cooked for him, made their modest council flat a warm place he longed to come home to. At times she apologised and desperately pleaded with Steve to leave her. She believed she wasn't worthy of love or that she had no love to give and it was better for Steve to find someone else.

About a year into their marriage, Freya began to share her past with Steve regarding her first marriage, and the death of both her husband and son. She spoke about her journey to England after she had been freed and then later to Scotland. She also briefly mentioned she had spent time off and on in several mental institutions. Steve came to realise that with all the traumas Freya had encountered and witnessed during the war, she would be haunted by the past for the rest of her life. After living with Freya, Steve discovered that her situation was never about being cured, but rather how to manage her depression and the self-harming thoughts that were never far from her mind.

Freya didn't want any children nor did she think she would be able to get pregnant again due to her age. So it was an understatement to say it took her totally by surprise when she discovered that she was going to have another baby. During her pregnancy, Freya still had moments when she would be disconnected, staring into space, but these symptoms and her self-harming tendency drastically decreased. It was the happiest they had ever been. Many evenings after their meal, they would sit in the living room listening to the radio, talking about their future and discussing names for the baby. Seeing his wife busy making clothes for the baby led Steve to be optimistic about their future. He convinced himself that all the trouble was behind them.

Their son George was born when Freya was forty-four years old. Steve was elated at the birth of their little son. He honestly thought that he would be a loner all his life, so it was beyond his wildest dreams when he'd got married and now he had become a father to a wee beautiful boy.

Freya took a prolonged maternity leave after the birth. She became extremely protective of little George. Each time Steve wanted to pick him up when he was crying Freya would criticise him for holding the baby incorrectly. Steve didn't challenge her and kept quiet, avoiding further arguments because he was afraid of putting Freya's mental state under strain. Nevertheless, he also noticed she would behave oddly at times, like when at night she would hold George for hours on end and wouldn't let go of him even in his sleep. Many times she would even purposely shake him from his deep slumber to make sure he was breathing.

One day on coming home after work, Steve was approached by a concerned neighbour at the entrance to their building. This neighbour and his wife, both retired, lived next door to Steve. The man told him about hearing the baby's frequent loud cries and voiced his concern that the child was being neglected. Apparently, when Steve was at work and Freya was alone with George, she would, at times, just let him cry his lungs out for long periods in his crib. Before he departed, the man told Steve that he would keep a close eye on the situation.

Steve was conflicted about the neighbour's warning and pondered whether or not to speak to Freya about it. He was consumed with worry that she would not take it well especially as it was an outsider criticising how she was taking care of their son. Steve didn't have to wait too long before things got worse. A week or so after their talk, the same neighbour banged on the door when George had again been crying non-stop for a long time. The man shouted through the door, asking what the matter was and threatening to call social services. Freya didn't answer the door, but the crying stopped.

Unknown to the neighbour, on the other side of the door, the banging and shouting had roused Freya from her deep thoughts. Holding George, she was at first confused about who this baby was. It was not the son she remembered. Memories of when she worked in the kitchen during her time in the concentration camp overwhelmed her. The trauma of inhaling hot air and smoke coming out from the camp's crematorium as the Nazis disposed of the bodies of those killed in the gas chambers haunted her. Images of war were racing through her mind of people running, fleeing from bombs with dead bodies all around, and she heard screams and cries. Suddenly, she was once again separated from her husband and her son snatched away from her, never to be seen again. A tumultuous panic started to grow in her head because the images of her husband and son were fading and she wasn't able to remember their faces.

"If you neglect your baby again I will report it to the social services. You hear me?" shouted the neighbour firmly through the letterbox on the door to make sure his message was clearly delivered before he finally went back to his home.

The neighbour's stern voice fully awakened Freya and she realised she was in her home in Edinburgh holding her new son, George, and she began crying and apologised to him profusely.

After the last intervention of the neighbour, the situation improved somewhat. Freya acted as if nothing had happened and didn't say anything to Steve about her encounters with their neighbour, not aware that he had already notified Steve about the problem.

Before George was two, during one of the regular periodic checks from the health visitor, it was discovered that he'd grown a lump on his right hip. Freya had failed to change George's terry towelling nappies frequently enough, at times forgetting completely. Due to the moisture trapped inside, a cyst grew. The case was reported back to the GP who swiftly scheduled an urgent operation. Worse yet, her GP and the social services evaluated the situation and decided George was to be sent to a foster family for a period of time after the operation. Freya pleaded and pleaded not to be separated from George not knowing her GP had already instructed her to be admitted to a mental institution again after reviewing the case and her file.

Steve was heartbroken having to witness not only his son being taken away but also his wife needing to be institutionalised once more. He blamed himself for being blind and not confronting Freya when the neighbour first alerted him. Maybe he had been too frightened to see and admit what was going on in his life with his little family. He felt as if he bore all the burdens of the world on his shoulders. He didn't talk to his colleagues because he didn't think anyone would understand his situation. He worked long hours to numb his pain, the only way he knew to deal with things. He was lost and felt he was totally alone, especially on returning to an empty home after work. The only joy that kept him going was his permitted visits to George in his provisional foster family and his wife in the mental institution, though both happened under supervision and during strictly scheduled time slots.

After a few months, Freya was released from the institution and Steve, much relieved, brought her home. Steve didn't tell Freya that the case was under evaluation concerning whether George was to be reunited with them for a trial period. He kept it a secret not wanting to disappoint her in the event of a negative result. On the other hand, he knew how much it would cheer her up in her still fragile state if George were to be united with them.

The day George was to be brought home, Steve told Freya he would be a bit later than usual as he needed to attend a work meeting. The whole day he couldn't help imagining the smile on Freya's face when she saw George and held him in her arms again.

When he got home with George, before opening the door he made a gesture with his finger on his mouth so George would understand to be quiet. George was now two and thought this was a fun game, playing along with the same gesture with his finger. They both failed to contain their excitement as they giggled. Steve was also carrying a bouquet of flowers he'd bought for Freya. He balanced the bouquet on one arm, holding George closer towards him and whispered "*Shhh*," in his ear to remind him once more to be quiet as he unlocked the door with excitement, holding his breath with suspense, and started to push it open.

"I'm home! Guess who is with me!" announced Steve at full volume and at the same time turning on the light in the hallway with his heart beating so fast his body was shaking.

At first, he saw a shadow in the dark and couldn't grasp clearly what was in the living room. Instinctively, an inkling crept into his head, a thought he had imagined in his darker moments but dreaded to acknowledge was a possibility. His legs weakened as he moved towards the indistinct shape in the darkness. He held his breath in suspense and with his trembling hand he turned on the main room light.

"NO!" Steve cried out in despair. He dropped the bouquet on the floor. The last thing he remembered doing that evening was holding on tight to George and turning his head away.

Freya had hanged herself from the ceiling.

Chapter 1 – 2021

"Sorry, but I'll need to go out to the deck," announced George, disrupting a conversation he realised he hadn't had the patience nor tolerance to follow. He offered an apologetic look, glancing around the table with a nod.

"Anything the matter? Are you all right, son?" wondered Aileen, eyeing George with concern about his sudden need to depart.

"Not to worry, Mum, I just need to get some fresh air," replied George, mumbling the words. He rose from the table, angling for the nearest exit. For a brief second, George hesitated as he felt he'd been overly dramatic and that maybe it seemed he was fleeing from the group. Then he remembered how they had referred to each other in front of Alastair and his wife Michelle and his urge to leave became more pressing. He felt suffocated and a wave of nausea engulfed him.

As George walked towards the exit he had to occasionally hold on to tables and pillars to gain his balance even though the ferry was only rocking lightly from the swell of the waves. All the time, he felt they were watching him as he struggled to walk with the weight he had evidently gained during the recent COVID lockdowns. He didn't turn back, though at that moment he realised he'd forgotten his jacket. He reached the exit, pushed the door open and was hit with cold air and a hint of sunshine despite this being in late autumn. As soon as he got out, he felt he was able to breathe easily again. He looked around the surroundings and saw that quite a lot of people were outside enjoying the view of the endless water as the ferry crossed the Pentland Firth heading for Orkney. He drew a long breath. It was then that he realised he hadn't brought his facial mask. He felt a bit uneasy as some people were still wearing theirs, even in the open air.

After a short while his thoughts went back to Aileen, the woman he had called Mum for as long as he could remember. But was she his mum? Wasn't it odd to call her that in front of Alastair, her real son? George closed his eyes, massaged his temples as sudden fatigue overcame him. For George, Aileen was the only mother he had. George had never known his birth mother nor had he any memories of her. George's father, Steve, had remarried Aileen, a divorcee, when George was about three, one year after the suicide of his birth mother. Aileen had been a great mum to George and loved him as her own.

Aileen was also a devoted wife to Steve and cared for him till he died roughly eight months ago at the end of 2020 during one of the lockdowns, a few months after turning eighty-seven. Steve was not an easy man to live with or please. He was a man with many flaws, often in a sullen mood, stingy, controlling and he loved to argue at all times to prove he was right. He was a heavy smoker till his late sixties. It was like pulling teeth when the doctor ordered him to take care of his diet when he had to give up his beloved pints and fry-ups. Ever since he was diagnosed with type two diabetes due to his earlier lifestyle, Aileen had to have his food and sugar intake monitored, which caused many arguments and required persuasion with patience from Aileen. Things had become particularly problematic five years before his passing since Steve also developed dementia. Aileen had looked after Steve all by herself until the last two years when it became too much for her, as they were both getting frail with age. With his dementia worsening, the only workable solution was having him stay in a care home, where he later died.

A few months after the funeral of Steve, once the travel quarantine restrictions had been lifted, Alistair and his wife Michelle travelled from California to Edinburgh to visit Aileen. Alastair, three years older than George, was her biological son from Aileen's first marriage to Ken Park. In 1968, when Alastair was about nine, the family, including his father's new wife and Alistair's half-siblings, emigrated to the US.

The new young Mrs Park's family had relatives operating hotels in the US and it was a great opportunity for them when an offer came up for Ken to invest, with the help of his new wife's parents, in a new hotel chain. She saw it as an unmissable opportunity to cut the tie with her in-laws for various reasons. She recognised potential in her husband but in her mind, he would never have achieved any kind of greatness if he were to remain under the tight control of his parents. At face value, the new young Mrs Park and her mother-in-law amiably tolerated each other but she shouldn't be mistaken for a pushover though. She would never allow her mother-in-law to rule their lives or make decisions about the upbringing of their children.

Aileen was heartbroken when she received the news. She tormented and blamed herself for Alistair leaving because she felt it was her fault to have lost him twice, once when she was forced out of their matrimonial home by her then mother-in-law and the second time when he moved to the US. Since then Aileen hadn't seen much of Alastair. At that time, transatlantic travel wasn't as convenient and affordable as these days. Their contact was irregular and not frequent, mainly because she was married to Steve and Steve wasn't fond of her having contact with Alastair. Also, it wasn't encouraged by Alastair's father either. Their relationship rekindled only when Alastair became a bit older.

Growing up, Alistair did visit Aileen a few times when he came back to Edinburgh to visit his paternal grandparents. Those meetings were arranged quietly and without the presence of Steve or George. Years later, Aileen also flew to the US to attend the wedding when Alastair married Michelle. Alastair and Michelle also came to Edinburgh a few times with their children, more frequently after the death of Alastair's father a few years back. Those trips and visits were never talked about openly in the home where she and Steve lived.

It had always been a dream of Aileen's that both her *sons* could become better acquainted. When Aileen first suggested this five-day bus tour trip together to visit Orkney from Edinburgh, George wasn't warm to the idea of spending such a long time with Alistair and his wife even though George had long wanted to visit many famous sites there, like the Italian Chapel and the stone circle at Brodgar. George wasn't able to pinpoint the reason for his hesitation but he felt rather uneasy travelling with Alistair and Michelle, the two he'd only got to know through photos at that stage. Another worry of his was he wasn't convinced that Aileen would be able to put herself through such a trip. After all, she had turned eighty-five.

"Exactly! She's now eighty-five. Is that too much to ask of you, to honour her wish before it's too late? Besides, didn't you mention many times your dream to visit the northeastern coast of Scotland?" asked Sarah, George's wife, shaking her head to show her dismay about his stubbornness, especially when George was vague about his concern. She'd tried numerous times to reason with her husband to agree to this trip ever since they'd received the invite from Aileen a few months ago. She didn't understand his reluctance or lack of interest. She so much hoped he would come to his senses because it would mean so much to her mother-in-law.

Much to Sarah's delight, the trip went ahead though she herself had to cancel and wasn't able to take part at the last minute. Sarah's father had unexpectedly died two weeks before the trip. After the funeral took place, she and her brother had to sort out his estate.

What a mess. I'm happy I don't need to get involved!
As George reflected, the bus tour seemed more attractive compared to the affair of sorting out Sarah's father's estate and dealing with her brother. He shook his head. From the sound of it, Sarah was taking a stand, which didn't sit well with her brother and that made George think that they would see less of him and his family. *Hope I no longer need to listen to his condescending and patronising talks about how I should manage my finances.*

The bus tour had left Edinburgh the previous morning, making stops at Stirling Castle and the Wallace Monument then Doune Castle, then crossing the Fault Line into the Highlands. The tour also visited Loch Ness and they spent their first night in Inverness. The next morning, they boarded the ferry in Gills Bay.

On the deck of the ferry, George looked up and around. People were coming out to enjoy the sight of the open water but more were going in due to the turning of the weather. He closed his eyes for a moment and thought about his marriage to Sarah; unconsciously it brought a smile to his face. Apart from Aileen, she was the most patient person he knew. A sudden feeling of guilt overcame him with the realisation that Sarah had been a good and supportive wife and truth be told, even George knew he hadn't been an easy person to live with. Besides making Aileen happy, another reason that prompted George to agree to participate in this trip was to give Sarah a bit of breathing space because frictions between them had intensified, largely during the lockdown periods when they were forced to live at home. Spending time together 24/7 was challenging, to say the least, for any relationship.

Aye, I should be more considerate towards her, after all, she's still grieving for the loss of her father.

George was miles away when he felt someone gently tapping on his shoulder.

"Aileen asked me to check on you."

George looked over his shoulder, turned and saw Alistair there.

George studied Alistair as he stood next to him. He didn't say anything because he was puzzled that Alistair had called his own mother by her name. *Is this an American thing? Or does he find it awkward to refer to her as Mum in front of me?* "Erm…"

"Are you sure you don't want to come in? Is everything OK?" asked Alistair, trying to read his facial expression. Alistair sensed George was contemplating something in his head.

"Oh, aye. I'll rejoin you guys in a short while. I just needed some fresh air," said George and squeezed a somewhat convincing smile without revealing his feelings.

"I thought you were maybe uncomfortable with the conversation? Have I offended you in anything I said? I thought we were just having a laugh," stated Alistair, hoping to clear the air.

George stared at Alistair in surprise at his directness and was uncertain how to respond. To break the awkward silence, George worked out he needed to say something quickly. "Not at all! I reckon I must have eaten too quickly; I had a bit of acid reflux. I feel much better now. Tell Mu... Tell her I'll be in soon." George offered an explanation, again keeping his emotions and feelings at bay. He was hoping Alistair would go back in and bloody leave him alone because he still needed a few more minutes for himself.

"Will do! Just wanted to be sure. It's getting chilly out here." Alistair held his arms across his chest, shivering through the cold.

"You've no jacket on either, you better get in! It's getting windy out here. I won't be long."

George followed Alistair with his eyes as he went back inside the cabin and started to think about the string of encounters he had had with Alistair and Michelle since they met up yesterday.

*

Aileen and George had spoken on the phone and agreed to meet in a café inside the bus terminal before they got on the tour bus. Alistair and Michelle had arrived five days prior to the trip and stayed with Aileen. They were all supposed to have dinner together at Aileen's for them to meet for the first time but Michelle had just recovered from a cold she picked up prior to their arrival which meant the dinner was cancelled.

Aileen, Alistair and Michelle arrived first. While waiting for George, Aileen had a smile across her face and appeared extremely pleased, anticipating the joy of the first trip with her two sons together.

George on the other hand was frustrated even before the trip for various reasons. He tried his best not to sound petty when he expressed his annoyance to Sarah before he left home about feeling like an outsider because Alistair and Michelle would have come together with Aileen. Then it turned out that Sarah wasn't able to join, knowing that he would be apprehensive about meeting Alistair and his wife for the first time and spending time with them. What troubled George the most was the anticipated awkwardness of interacting with Aileen in the presence of Alistair and Michelle.

"Good morning, son, here are Alistair and Michelle." Aileen waved and greeted George when she saw him approaching the table where she, Alistair and Michelle sat. Aileen was positively glowing, well content with this special occasion.

Bewildered, fiddling with his hand, George was still digesting and adjusting to everything when, without any hesitation, Alistair stood up, came forward and gave George a warm hug, followed by Michelle.

After the greetings, George had a chance to take a quick glance at them. Even though Aileen had shown him and Sarah photos of Alistair and Michelle, for whatever inexplicable reason, George had a mental image of them as JR Ewing and Sue Ellen Ewing, two of the main characters from the American '80s hit TV show *Dallas*. Even though they were not from Texas, George even pictured Alistair wearing a cowboy hat and Michelle with big hair and large shoulder pads.

Unlike Aileen, Alistair was tall, almost a head taller than George and had red hair and intense blue eyes. Michelle had similar short greyish hair like Aileen's, a hairstyle that Aileen had found comfortable in recent years. Although they were older than George, they were both in much better shape, with nice suntans and, the trademark of Americans, perfectly straight and porcelain white teeth. Alistair and Michelle didn't wear anything expensive or flashy from what George could tell but their whole appearance and the way they carried themselves made George feel inadequate and insecure. In his head, they must have noticed his pale skin and the weight he had put on in recent years and, not to mention, his two missing teeth at the side of his mouth, exposed whenever he spoke and smiled.

Wonder if those perfect straight teeth are really their own? As George thought about the question it somehow made him less inferior, a bit. He had a smirk on his face at the idea but it was soon wiped off when he introspectively considered his own behaviour and became filled with a sense of shame. He quickly realised it was such a cheap shot, making a personal attack on their appearance, and his assumptions about them were unfounded and none of his business.

"Here, something we brought from the US for your daughter Kimberly's children," happily announced Michelle with a self-contented giggle and handed George a bag of gifts.

"Cheers. Oh, that's very thoughtful of you! Now I feel bad because I didn't buy anything for yours," said George, visibly uncomfortable. He turned his head and looked at Aileen for help.

"Don't worry about it. We would love to meet Kimberly and her family one day. Sorry about Sarah's father. Please send our condolences to her." Michelle pulled out chairs for them while Alistair went to get drinks.

"I will. Much appreciated. And, thanks for these," said George, pointing at the gift bag.

They all enjoyed their first sip of their hot beverage and felt more relaxed. They started discussing this trip while enthusiastically studying the trip itinerary they had received from the tour operator. At that point, for the first time, George felt optimistic about this trip but that amicable feeling didn't last long.

"Mum, you must come and live with us! You would love the weather in California. I know I was born here and I appreciate my Scottish roots but America is the greatest country in the world!" declared Alistair with his overpowering tone, keenly looking at Aileen for an answer.

Aileen just smiled but didn't seem to be over-awed by Alistair's suggestion. George raised his eyebrows with the suspicion that it was not the first time they'd had this conversation. He kept quiet pondering about Alistair's claim about America being the greatest country in the world. *Yes, America is a great country but what does it mean to be the greatest country in the world? Says who?*

I'm damn glad to be living in Scotland. In my opinion, the UK National Health Service is the best in the world, affordable and accessible to everyone, particularly for those residing in Scotland.

"It's time. I reckon we'd better get ready for boarding the bus," said Aileen while finishing her coffee. She gently tapped twice on George's hand as she saw he seemed to be totally absorbed in his thoughts from the facial expressions he was displaying. "I'm glad you're here son." She leaned closer and discretely whispered in his ear.

They gathered their luggage and got inside the bus and started their tour where the minibus driver, who was also the tour guide, welcomed the group of ten through the on-board speaker system.

"Now I've told you a bit about myself and about the tour. Could you make a short introduction about yourself, your name, where are you from and why are you visiting Orkney?" encouraged the tour guide.

One could hear giggles and laughs as the presentation went around the group.

After George briefly talked about himself he heard an assertive voice come over his shoulder from behind. He realised it was Alistair.

"I'm Alistair and I'm here with my wife Michelle. I was born in Scotland and moved to California, US, when I was quite young. We're here visiting my mum who lives in Edinburgh. We heard about lots of interesting sites in Orkney and are really looking forward to visiting them."

"And, we'll become grandparents again next month! Our daughter is due to give birth to our third grandchild!" Michelle added.

"Congratulations!" the group cheered.

"Welcome home to Scotland, and congratulations. Erm, so, what do you think of your current president?" Out of nowhere, the tour guide burst in with an enthusiastic question.

"We didn't vote for him," Alistair immediately offered a firm and short response.

With that, the atmosphere suddenly changed; George could be wrong but was almost certain that at that moment the answer surprised most of the people on the bus, not to mention the guide who'd posed the question.

They made a few touristic stops and in the late afternoon, then they reached Inverness as the first major stop of their trip. As soon as he checked in to their hotel and was in his room alone he called Sarah to report.

"Alistair said he didn't vote for Biden. But, what did he mean he didn't vote for him? He didn't vote at all in the last election or he voted differently?" George moaned under his breath to make sure Aileen or Alistair staying in the same hotel a few doors down would not hear.

"What an inappropriate question for the tour guide to ask! The guide shouldn't have put them in such an awkward situation." Sarah was appalled. She thought the guide had acted utterly unprofessionally and was rather cross with George for dwelling on this matter.

"I'm so shocked. I—"

"Why? They're entitled to their opinion and political stance like everyone else. You wouldn't want anyone else to comment on yours, would you?" Sarah jumped in and gave George a mouthful expressing her dismay, with a hint of frustration creeping into her tone.

George squinted his face. Knowing her view on this matter, he was surprised and rather disappointed that Sarah didn't share his line of thinking. He became quiet for a moment restlessly flipping the night table light switch while contemplating what to say. "Aye, but I thought you—"

"George, don't waste your time in other people's business. Who are you to judge? You don't know their circumstances. Try to enjoy the trip, at least for Aileen." Without wasting any time Sarah cut George off again.

After the talk with Sarah, he wasn't able to relax in his room. George dreaded the idea of meeting Aileen, Alistair and Michelle for dinner. Thankfully they only had a quick bite to eat because they were all tired from an early start in the morning. They all agreed on an early night.

Before George fell asleep, he was still in two minds about the incident. The thought of Alistair and Michelle not voting for the current president made his stomach turn. Then he thought about what Sarah said. *They had every right to their political views so why should it have bothered me so much who they voted for?* But he was still uneasy about what he'd just learned. It had troubled him and he found it hard to let it go.

The next morning, they continued on the second day of the tour with an early start as well. They drove along the northeast Highland coastline reaching Scotland's most northerly mainland village, John o'Groats, and then on to Gills Bay where they boarded the ferry heading to Orkney.

After they had first got on the ferry, Alistair and George queued to buy lunch in the ferry cafeteria while Aileen and Michelle sat down. At the till, Alistair held his credit card in one hand and stretched out the other to prevent George from moving forward then heavy-handedly put it atop George's wallet.

With a wink he said in a loud voice, "No, no, it's on me! Your money is not good here! You can help me carry the trays," affirmed Alistair without noticing George cocking an eyebrow, finding his gesture somewhat insulting and patronising. He hated the way Alistair flashed his money and credit card around, acting like he owned the whole damned world.

"Here. Hope this will do for now. Will take you out for a nice meal this evening." Alistair placed a paper cup of carrot and coriander soup and a napkin containing a piece of bread in front of Aileen and Michelle.

While eating their rather simple lunch, Michelle and Alistair were telling George about their new life in California as winemakers as well as showing him quite a large collection of photos of their children and grandchildren.

George had to bite his lip and disguise his boredom a few times. For the sake of Aileen and not to make a scene, he politely looked through all the photos and occasionally made positive remarks. After a while, George was already exhausted as he considered Alistair to be showing off. Soon George became practically bored to death when Alistair talked nonstop about the organic vineyard they had recently acquired since they'd retired. It was even worse when Alistair started explaining specific terminologies about organic wine farming and their new lifestyle as vegans, two topics that would never have interested George.

To make the matter even more unbearable, he started to get irritated about Michelle's laugh, which in his ears sounded like a broken record mating with a blow horn. *How could a petite person make such a loud noise?* He wondered if people around were staring at their table. Without being aware of it, George's dislike of Michelle being loud in public was the same thing his wife and daughter constantly teased him about. He was so occupied mentally criticising Alistair and Michelle that he omitted to ask himself the question of whether he was the one who had been judgemental and over-sensitive about everything they said and did.

As his irritation grew he also thought about the expensive gifts Alistair and Michelle had bought for his grandchildren, a silver bracelet and necklace each from Tiffany. *So unnecessary. Are they expecting me to buy something pricey in return for their grandchildren?*

While George was mulling over his thoughts, the conversation somehow switched to gossiping about celebrities and then to the still much-talked-about event –

Meghan and Prince Harry's interview with Oprah Winfrey, which had just been aired a few months earlier. Alistair and Michelle expressed their opinion about the interview and how it was distasteful and disrespectful towards the Royal Family, specifically in some of the unfounded claims raised by Meghan.

"It can't be that bad. Someone in the Royal Family questioned the skin colour of their child. I'm sure it was just a light-hearted comment. Why do they have to turn everything into a racial matter? These people are always playing the victim. She's just over the top and being self-righteous! They must know they've burnt their bridges after this interview." Alistair threw his hands in the air expressing his dismay while Michelle nodded her head fiercely in agreement.

While watching Alistair spitting out his opinions, George avoided eye contact with Aileen because it must have been as awkward for her as it was for him for obvious reasons.

Sarah and George had watched the interview together and they didn't see anything wrong with Prince Harry and his wife revealing their views. They felt, however, that it was unfortunate that it resulted in such negative attention and reactions, like the one Alistair and Michelle were having.

Sarah had been fascinated by the Royal Family ever since she could remember. She heard once from a pupil in school as a little girl that the Royal Family don't need to go to the toilet and she'd believed it for a long, long time. Sarah found out somehow that on the day in

September 2015, the Queen became the longest reigning British sovereign and that the Queen and Prince Philip would be at the Waverley train station in Edinburgh. She took a day off from work and accompanied Aileen and Steve to be in the crowds greeting them. It was an event they all cherished and talked often about. Apart from their respect for the Queen, George, Sarah and Aileen always had a soft spot for Prince Harry due to their love for the late Lady Diana. They sympathised with the pain he carried about how his mother had been betrayed and badly treated by people around her and particularly by the press before her tragic death.

For George, the limit had been reached. He just wasn't able to sit there listening to more mockeries coming from Alistair, so he left the conversation. George took it to heart and felt Alistair was attacking Prince Harry and Meghan for no reason other than making fun of them without understanding their side of the story.

On the way to the deck, he asked himself when it had become an acceptable norm to criticise and bully Meghan based on perceptions about her? Is it right that the media and the general public do not consider the burden placed on their mental health and well-being? While George was boiling inside, he failed to recognise the reason behind his own overreaction and sensitivity towards this issue.

George's daughter Kimberly was married to Cameron who had been born in the UK to immigrant parents. Sarah told George once what she learned from Kimberly about how much verbal and invisible abuse Cameron and his parents had endured due to their ethnicity and his parents' noticeable accent when speaking English. What was even more hurtful was that since their children were mixed race, Kimberly and Cameron had also been on the receiving end of so-called 'light-hearted' remarks about their children's skin colour and their looks. Worse of all, his own father, Steve, had also made comments about Cameron after Kimberly first introduced him to Aileen and himself. Luckily, Steve didn't say it directly to Kimberly or Sarah and those remarks were shut down quickly by Aileen and George. George remembered exactly his father defensively saying with a cheeky expression each time he'd been confronted, "Oh, don't be so over-dramatic about it! It was just a joke and I didn't mean anything by it."

With time, Steve had accepted Cameron and would fight to the last if anyone would say anything about him or his children with Kimberly, though Steve still voiced his opinions and prejudices about immigrants and gay people. Till today those borderline discriminative and degrading remarks of his father still hurt George, so he understood from first-hand experience how hurtful it must be for Meghan and Prince Harry when however 'light-hearted' comments were unfairly made towards them and their child.

*

"Excuse me! I need to pass."

Suddenly, he felt a pain in his arm which brought him back from his reverie and at the same time, he heard a voice from someone approaching him and squeezing past him in order to get inside. The man collided with George as he lost his balance and accidentally bumped into him. George moaned silently in pain and reflexively grasped his right arm with his left hand. He furrowed his brow. His arm had been sore after his second vaccine booster shot a few days ago. He'd had a bad reaction experiencing sore arm and fatigue, worse than the first one.

For fuck's sake. Watch where you're going. You didn't even care to apologise. George was in agony seeing the man clumsily enter the cabin.

ATISHOO! George sneezed. *I'd better get inside as well. It's getting cold.* As George was heading back to his group, he prayed the rest of the trip wouldn't be too dreadful and unbearable.

Much to his delight, in the end, George surprisingly came around and was able to pull himself out of his self-pity, pull the metaphorical stick out of his behind and stop being constantly offended. Having said that, he still felt uneasy and self-conscious around Alistair and Michelle because of the complexity of his emotions and the feeling that every time they looked at him they would see a fraud, the inauthentic son of Aileen. His anxieties and frustrations waned each time he thought about what Sarah had pointed out. The least he could do was to make an effort for Aileen's sake, the woman who'd raised him and loved him, who had never asked for anything in return.

The days went quicker than George had imagined. One moment they were boarding the ferry heading to Orkney and the next he was already saying his goodbyes to Aileen, Alistair and Michelle at the bus station back in Edinburgh.

On his way home, he was secretly thinking he wouldn't mind if the trip were a bit longer. He was also excited contemplating what he was going to tell his wife about the beautiful scenery in Orkney and how much he'd needed this trip because it was his first time away from Edinburgh since the horrendous pandemic saga and all the associated restrictions had started. Not to mention the beaming smile he saw on Aileen's face throughout the whole trip.

"I'm glad I survived the trip!" complained George to Sarah once he got home and was stunned as soon as those words left his own mouth, totally the opposite of what he had in mind.

"I'm sure it was not even half as bad as you made out to be!" Sarah teased.

"You weren't there so it's easy for you to say," George grumbled and handed Sarah the gift bag he'd received from Alistair and Michelle for Kimberly's children.

Sarah shook her head. She knew her husband too well and realised that he was too proud to acknowledge to her that he did in fact, enjoy the trip and that in his head if he admitted this it would make him a lesser man.

"See, they're so thoughtful. I don't understand you. Why do you make it so difficult for yourself?" remarked Sarah while appraising the gifts.

"You don't understand!" George mumbled shaking his head. He didn't share his thoughts of his inferiority with Sarah. His mindset was that he would rather have her blaming him for not liking them than having to reveal his true insecurities.

"I was thinking of inviting them over for dinner before their departure," said Sarah in a serious tone, though she was betrayed by the twinkles in her eyes. She burst into laughter.

"Don't even joke about it. It's not funny," exclaimed George, though he felt bad for Aileen. He knew she had tried her best for the 'two brothers' to form a bond or at least get along, but it was a wild goose chase on George's side. His take was that it was best if he didn't have to see them again. With him feeling so insecure, encounters with Alistair and Michele had troubled him from the first time they had met. As obnoxious as it might be, he just couldn't shake off the thought that they saw him as the fake son, a substitute.

Sarah might only have been joking about having dinner but someone else had had the same idea as well.

A few days prior to Alistair and Michelle returning to California, Aileen organised a dinner. Sarah happily accepted the invitation for her and George, which angered him because she hadn't checked with him.

"What is the matter with you?" Sarah scolded him. "It would make Aileen very happy. Also, they're leaving soon, remember!"

George didn't engage in further discussion. He had his own cunning plan. In his opinion, there was always a last resort of playing the 'not feeling well card' on the day of the dinner, and in fact, he did just that.

"Dad, there is nothing wrong with you. Don't act like a child," Kimberly confronted George over the phone straight away when Sarah told her about her father's tantrum. She'd called Kimberly for help when she wasn't able to convince him to go.

"Stop ganging up on me," George protested, giving an unpleasant look at Sarah who happened to be standing next to him, giggling.

"You know how disappointed Nan would be if you didn't go. You're going and that is that," ordered Kimberly.

In the end, George attended the dinner along with Sarah. With a strict warning from Sarah, he was told to be on his best behaviour with good manners. In order to avoid hearing further reminders from Sarah and also out of his respect towards Aileen, George, believe it or not, did behave and even enjoyed the evening. Without much effort, he contributed to conversations and laughed at jokes, not just to be sociable but because it was quite pleasant, as it turned out.

"It wasn't that bad, was it?" asked Sarah when they'd left Aileen's after dinner and were waiting for the bus home.

George didn't reply. Partly it was because he was busy studying the timetable for the next bus but also because he wasn't certain what Sarah meant. Whether she was referring to meeting Alistair and Michelle again or to the vegan dinner prepared by Michelle. He had a silent burp and gently stroked his belly; it made a rumbling sound. His stomach did not agree with lentils and tofu and also as far as he could remember he'd never had a meal without eating meat.

"Oh, look!" said Sarah, pointing at the moon and admiring the sight.

"*Hmm.*" From the corner of his eye, George had a quick peek at the direction Sarah was pointing. He mumbled something incoherent in a sombre mood.

"They seemed very nice. Alistair is very tall. He must be taking after his father," Sarah offered her impression of Alistair and Michelle and continued with her chit-chat. "Oh, it's freezing." She blew out a cold breath and shivered. She crossed her arms and rubbed herself vigorously.

George remained silent because he was too frustrated to have a conversation. Frustrated that he felt petty for not warming up more to Alistair and Michelle, at the same time, as far as he was concerned, he'd rather not be forced and reciprocate a friendship that didn't exist.

"If there is any consolation, now you can finally say that you don't need to see them again, at least for a long while. Get your bus pass ready. It's arriving soon," Sarah alerted George with a nudge to his arm and reached inside her handbag for her own bus pass. "I'm beat!" Sarah yawned.

Chapter 2 – 2021

It was one month after their trip to Orkney. George had come to visit Aileen, by himself.

"Thanks for coming. No sugar, right? Or would you prefer tea?" Aileen smiled and offered George a cup of coffee as he sat down on the sofa in the living room.

"Ta." George smiled back about the no-sugar comment as he'd been half-heartedly trying to lose weight. For a few moments, George quietly enjoyed his coffee, contemplating the reason Aileen had invited him over to speak to him. On many occasions, George used to come to see Steve and Aileen without Sarah, back when Steve was alive. He also visited Aileen alone after Steve died so he was bewildered about her specific request that he come without his wife.

"Has Sarah upset you?" asked George when Aileen first mentioned over the phone that she wanted to see him, just him.

"How could Sarah have upset me? Not at all. Just something I need to run past you alone," assured Aileen, surprised by George's idea.

An opportunity arose and George had called Aileen to inform her that he could come over one afternoon in the next few days. Sarah just confirmed her trip to Aberdeen to stay with their daughter Kimberly and her family for a few days. Kimberly had studied in Aberdeen and had remained there when she met her future husband, Cameron. They now had two children and were operating a nursery.

After the initial small talk, Aileen and George sat silently for a while. Both were preoccupied with their own thoughts. It was as though they were each waiting for the other to start the conversation. George gazed around the living room of this one-story bungalow and thought about his childhood home.

When Steve and Aileen got married, Aileen moved in with Steve and George to their small council flat, a third-floor place without lifts. A little over one year later, some blocks of council flats in various parts of Edinburgh were turned into private homes, including theirs. All the residents living there were offered the chance to buy either their own or other unoccupied ones at a discounted price. It just happened that Aileen had inherited money from her father after his passing so she and Steve were able to put that in addition to their savings towards the deposit to purchase a larger council flat in a different area in Edinburgh. This was the flat that George had called his childhood home. They sold it about twenty years ago and moved into this bungalow.

Though he often visited the bungalow and even spent a few nights there during holidays or after a night out, it was never his home. He still had difficulties figuring out all the light switches in some rooms. As he looked closer, he saw part of the wallpaper was discoloured and torn.

He placed his hand on the surface of the sofa and felt the worn fabric in some places.

"Dear, do you want more? Or a Coke?" Aileen finally broke the silence.

"No, no, I'm grand." Shaking his head fiercely, George wondered if Aileen had seen him daydreaming.

"Greetings from Alistair and Michelle by the way. I spoke to them two days ago," Aileen cheerfully reported.

"Oh, thanks. Say hi back to them for me."

"You know, seeing you both together had been a dream of mine for many years. I never thought it would be possible."

"Sure. I'm happy that you can now spend more time with him and his family."

Then they both fell into silence again chewing over in their mind their own thoughts.

While George was pondering his relationship with Alistair and Michelle, Aileen was preoccupied too, recalling something that had happened back in 1967 that had engraved itself in her memory and put such a dent in her heart that she had never forgiven herself, an incident that might have caused her not to be able to see Alistair for many years.

*

"Glad you could join our little group. Hope you've enjoyed our crochet gathering today!" The event host, Fiona, offered a cup of tea to Aileen after everyone had left while Aileen was waiting for Steve to come with George to drop him off before heading to a pub.

"Yes, I really enjoyed it! It's great to be getting to know new people, in particular since we've just moved to this area." Aileen smiled at Fiona and took a sip of the tea.

After they had all moved to the area, Aileen had joined the crochet and knitting group; it had always been Aileen's dream to learn how to crochet and knit. She figured it was also a way to find some new friends.

"When are they—" Fiona was interrupted by the doorbell. "Sorry, I'll be right back." She went to open the door.

"Hi! I'm Steve, Aileen's husband."

"Come in, come in. Aileen is in the kitchen waiting for you." Then Fiona saw a wee lad shyly standing next to Steve. With an animated voice she asked, "And you, you must be George. Your mum told me what a sweet wee boy you are." Fiona reached for George's hand and guided them both into the kitchen.

As soon as George saw Aileen, he went and hid behind her, looking at Fiona with a cheeky grin.

"George, come say hello to Fiona." Aileen gently pulled George from her back.

"George, say hello," ordered Steve with his firm voice, staring intensely at him.

Fiona looked at George with a friendly wink. "Don't worry. He'll warm up to me. How old is he?" Fiona turned towards Steve, distracting him from being too grating towards George.

48

"He's four and a half... He's a big boy now." It was Aileen who answered. She took out some sweets from her bag and gave them to George, who was now standing next to her, holding her hand.

"Would you like to be a boy scout one day? You can join starting at age six," Fiona enthusiastically suggested and gave George a gentle smile.

George lowered his head and crept behind Aileen again because he didn't like the attention being drawn to him, while both Steve and Aileen nodded waiting for Fiona to explain further.

"My husband is a boy scout sub-team leader in this area and both our boys have joined. I think it would be fun for George. My husband should be back soon with our boys. Why don't you wait a bit?"

"Aileen, why don't you stay and find out more, I'm in a bit of a rush. I've to..." Steve stopped and looked over his shoulder as he was distracted by the opening of the kitchen door.

"Hello, we're home!" announced a man, opening the kitchen door. He was tall and wore a country cap. He whistled as he entered. Following him were a few boys, full of beans and chatting and joking with each other, with a skip in their steps.

"Wipe your feet first!" Fiona pointed at their footwear and then made a stop signal with her hand before they barged in.

With an introduction from Fiona, Aileen learnt the man was her husband and the first two boys were their sons who had brought along a friend they met at a chess club that they'd recently joined.

Aileen gave a smile and a nod at Fiona's husband and took a quick glance at the boys after they entered the house. Suddenly she froze when she noticed the last boy with striking ginger hair was Alistair, her own son. He was wearing a sweater she'd bought him the last time they met, a sweater she specially chose for him as blue was his favourite colour.

Who would have thought that the paths of Fiona's family and Alistair would cross! For a brief moment, she was stunned and speechless. She noticed Alistair saw her as well. Her heart was beating so fast she thought it was going to jump out. She was extremely hot and flustered but knew she'd have to act normal before anyone suspected anything. With a quick stare from Aileen somehow Alistair understood not to approach her and call to her in front of everyone because it would have put his mother in an awkward position. Steve on the other hand was busy talking to Fiona's husband while Fiona sensed there was tension in the air but wasn't able to put her finger on it.

It broke Aileen's heart as Alistair was only about seven at that time and was sensitive beyond his age. Evidently, his parents' divorce made him more observant of what was happening around him. Intuitively, when Alistair saw his mother there with another man and a child he recognised, he understood they were her new family. After Aileen got remarried, Alistair asked his mother a few times to see a photo of George and reluctantly she showed it to him once, briefly. When he saw the photo of George, he would have loved to get to know him because Aileen told him that George also called her mummy, just like he was instructed to call his father's new wife.

After his father remarried, Alistair was made aware not to talk about his real mummy at home, specifically in front of his new mummy. The name of Aileen was never mentioned in their house as though she didn't exist. However, it was not totally true. His paternal grandmother, Mrs Park Senior, planted in his head more than once when they were alone that his mother had done some unforgivably bad things and was asked to leave their home. He was too young to properly understand, like what unforgivably bad things could there be? He loved his grandmother but one thing he was certain of was that he loved his mummy more. So in that moment, with a look from his mother, he knew he had to protect her. He played along with not knowing her.

Luckily, the boys didn't stay long in the kitchen. They all ran upstairs to play. But the guilt and shame that weighed on Aileen's shoulders were more than any pain she could imagine ever experiencing.

Aileen had no recollection of what had happened after that or how she even got home that afternoon. She did, however, remember that after putting George to bed and lying in bed next to Steve, who was snoring and drunk, her tears flooded silently in the dark. Thoughts kept lingering in her head, what a terrible mother she was; not even able to introduce herself as Alistair's mum in front of the others. She was heartbroken. She dreaded to think what her ex-husband Ken and his mother would say if they were to find out about what happened. She kept the incident to herself because she was too ashamed to admit what had happened. In her mind what could she have said for others to understand her pain and grasp her agony as a failed mother?

After that incident Aileen longed for a heart-to-heart talk with her son, to let him know how sorry she was. The next time they met up in Aileen's mother's place, Aileen found a moment alone with Alistair. She held back her tears crouching down to the same height and holding his hands remorsefully. She looked him right in the eyes and apologised to him and asked for his forgiveness. Alistair shook his head fiercely and assured her it didn't bother him. Leaning forward Alistair put arms tightly around his mother. He then rested his head on her shoulder and moved his hand around lightly on her back. He felt the warmth of her body with the familiar scent of hers; a scent that had made him cry on many nights in bed because he missed it.

"I'm sorry, I'm sorry, I'm sorry..." Aileen repeated as she sobbed.

Trying to comfort her, Alistair cried out, and his voice cracked as he hugged her tightly and wouldn't let go. "Mummy, Mummy, don't worry I won't tell anyone about it." Both of them burst into tears. In that moment, Alistair let his emotions loose, not needing to hide them out of concern for anyone else's opinion, as he was often caught between all the adults in his life.

*

"Ahem." After George pulled a lint ball from his sweater, he cleared his throat to break the silence. He was worried about Aileen because he could read from her facial expression that she was deeply agitated about whatever was troubling her. "Mum, is there something bothering you?"

"Oh, I'm a bit preoccupied. I was thinking about the first time you and Alistair met when you were younger," Aileen mumbled, her mind evidently still caught in her own thoughts.

"When? What do you mean?"

"Oh, nothing. I was just… never mind. You must be wondering why I wanted to speak to you?" said Aileen as she patted and adjusted a cushion and put it behind her back. She then sat up straight, ready to convey her message.

George nodded, waiting for Aileen to continue.

"I'm asking for your permission and forgiveness," she pleaded in a quavering voice. She put both hands across her face and her upper body started trembling.

This sudden outpouring of emotion caught George off guard. "Mum, I don't understand! What are you talking about? Why do you need my forgiveness and permission? For what?" Looking at Aileen, George's heart ached to see her so upset. He moved to sit closer to her and placed a hand on her shoulder.

What's wrong? I've never seen her so upset. Is she unwell?

"This has been troubling my mind for a while now and I feel so conflicted about what I'm about to ask you!" Aileen dried her tears with a tissue she took out from her sleeve. She blew her nose and took a deep breath, holding it in for a while before letting it out.

George saw that Aileen had calmed down so he shifted back to where he was sitting before. He adjusted the cushion before sitting down again and patiently waited for her. With his eyebrows furrowed, George remained concerned and puzzled.

Not able to look George in the eye, Aileen stared at the ceiling lamp because she found it easier to unveil her burden that way. "As you know, I married your dad when you were about three. I fell in love with you the first time I saw you and we quickly formed a bond. My heart melted when you first called me 'mummy'. I loved and raised you as my own and have never thought of being anything else than your mum." With a pause, Aileen reached for a glass of water and took a sip.

George looked at Aileen who was now tenderly looking at him as well. Aileen *was* his mum and the only mother he knew. George recalled fond memories of growing up with her; Steve wasn't a hands-on father or a man to show affection, so George associated such feelings primarily with Aileen.

"My ex-husband and his new family moved to the US in 1968 when Alistair was about nine. I wish I'd fought to keep him here. But how could I? I was remarried to your dad." Shaking her head, Aileen became silent again.

"Mum, let me get you some more?" said George, pointing at Aileen's empty glass. He went to the kitchen to get a refill and came back still puzzled over where Aileen was heading with her conversation. "Here." He handed her the glass.

"Ta." Aileen took another sip and continued, "After they moved to the US, we hardly had any contact for a few years. When he became older, we managed to write to each other. Letters were sent to my mother's address and I would write back to an address I understood was Alistair's best friend."

Aileen didn't need to explain to George, who knew the situation and his father too well, why letters were not sent to their own address where they lived.

As Aileen took another pause to catch her breath, George came to understand that what Aileen was about to tell him had something to do with Alistair. Yet he wondered why Aileen was keeping him in suspense and would not come straight to the point.

"I... I would like to include Alistair in my will as well." In the end, Aileen found the courage and as those words left her mouth her shoulders dropped in relief.

Looking at Aileen, George bit his lip and found himself tongue-tied as he was uncertain how to respond to this. Thoughts and questions entered his mind. *Why is she telling me this?*

As George didn't respond or react to what Aileen said she interpreted it as him being displeased.

"But, you and Kimberly will remain in my will. I'll divide things equally among you three," Aileen announced, her tone letting George know her well-meant intentions and not wanting to offend him.

"Mum, you didn't need to ask for my permission or worry about it," quickly responded George to reassure Aileen.

His initial thought was that it was her money and she could do whatever she wanted with it. Then an uncomfortable notion overcame him. *I wish she hadn't told me. But why give anything to Alistair, it's not like he or his children need money?*

From spending time with Alistair and Michelle in Orkney, George had learned that 'as a hobby' they purchased a manageable vineyard where they enjoyed their early retirement. Before that, they had managed a successful hotel chain business, which they inherited from Alistair's father. Not long ago they had passed the business on to their eldest. Their other children were successful in their own right.

"Thank you for your understanding. Alistair is quite comfortable financially and most likely does not expect anything from me, not that it'll be a significant amount! For me, it's just a token to show him that I'm his mother and that I feel guilty about not being around when he grew up," explained Aileen, looking at George seeking his understanding and not noticing the talk about the division of her will had led to inner turmoil for George.

"Mum, I'm certain Alistair would really appreciate the gesture. I'm sure, like me, Kimberly will also be honoured to be included in your will," said George with a calm tone trying his best not to let his sudden emotions of envy and jealousy towards Alistair show.

To comfort Aileen, George leaned forward, reached out and placed his hand atop hers. His annoyance faded as soon as he felt the warmth of her hand. As she aged, her hand had become covered in liver spots and had shrunk with many visible veins. But for George, her hands had always been strong and provided him with security and love. With them, she'd fed him, cared for him, raised him, cuddled him, supported and protected him.

Aileen had been the rock in his life for many reasons. Apart from George's affection towards her, Sarah and Kimberly also saw her as the glue of the family. Kimberly had a strong bond with Aileen and her kids called her Nan-Nan and she was an important figure in their lives.

Due to malnutrition and the inhuman treatment during her time spent in the concentration camp George's birth mother, Freya, had been extremely slim even throughout her pregnancy and that resulted in George being tiny and borderline too thin when he was born. He remained small and fragile for a long time, which caused him to become an insecure child growing up and Aileen was the one who had always been there for him through thick and thin. In contrast to Aileen, his father was never warm or loving towards him. Growing up, George felt as if he was always skating on thin ice around him. George adored Aileen and was very attached to her, which at times angered Steve because he saw George as being too needy. He didn't like seeing George clinging on to Aileen, as he saw it, rather than playing with other kids in the neighbourhood or from school. He sometimes used to dismissively call George 'Mummy's boy'.

"Son, you can't imagine how pleased I am!".

After hearing no objection from George to her suggestion about dividing her will, Aileen seemed relieved at the outcome of their conversation and her mood picked up. They then laughed as Aileen started to bring up some of the memorable mischief of George growing up. Although George was heading for sixty in two years, he enjoyed those mum-and-son moments.

"I still remember how nervous you were when you brought home your first girlfriend to meet your father and me. What was—" Aileen stopped as the phone rang and she reached for it and saw it was from Kimberly.

While Aileen spoke to Kimberly on the phone George reflected on the day's conversation and that led him in turn to think about his father and Aileen's financial situation.

Both George and Kimberly received a reasonable amount in cash inheritance after the death of Steve. Steve and Aileen had been careful with their money. One could even say that Steve was borderline frugal except for two things. One was what he spent at the pub and then what he contributed to a life insurance policy. Credit to him, he had always been keen on building up a life insurance premium throughout his adult life, which his funeral was mostly covered by. In Steve's will, the majority of his estate went to Aileen including the bungalow, which was paid off. There was also a portion of his pension that she was entitled to.

George had never thought about Aileen's estate or her will till she brought it up that day because he never considered he'd have any right to say how Aileen should divide her estate the day she passed away. Nevertheless, he felt uneasy now knowing that Alistair would receive something from the money his father and Aileen had saved throughout their whole lives.

As he looked at Aileen talking to Kimberly, George's mind slipped down memory lane to an event that had taken place in 1970 when he was about seven, when he found out about his birth mother for the first time.

*

One day at school during lunch break, George was about to leave the playground to go to the toilet when he noticed a few pupils a couple of grades above him whispering to each other and looking at him in an unfriendly fashion.

At first, George ignored them but as their laughter continued he took a quick glance at them.

"What are you looking at?" said one of the pupils in a challenging tone.

George felt uncomfortable about the situation. He looked straight ahead and tried not to pay attention to them. He continued walking though his action only angered the group further.

"Hey, Georgie boy, your mother was crazy and was locked in a loony bin before she killed herself!" one kid shouted out and the others all giggled. When they saw George was embarrassed and confused, they laughed louder pointing at him.

George stopped turned back and shouted at them, "That is not true! My mother didn't kill herself," anger flashing in his eyes. He was surprised by his courage in talking back to them as they were older and bigger than he was. He didn't understand what they were talking about but no one should talk about his mother that way. *How could his mother have killed herself? She'd just dropped him off at school this morning. What did they mean she was in a loony bin?* At that age, he didn't fully grasp what it meant but he was aware it must be something unpleasant, indicated by their smirking laughter.

An assistant teacher who happened to be standing nearby heard what had been said and intervened. She quickly came to George's aid and told the other kids to behave.

The assistant teacher took George's hand, trying to lead him inside but George wasn't moving. He stood with his feet planted firmly on the ground. He looked angrily up at the woman craving an answer from her.

"My dear, it's best you talk to your father and mother. Come along; let's go inside," she said in a calm tone, disguising her anger towards those other boys.

After they went inside, the assistant teacher reported it to the headmaster of the school who then promptly called Aileen at work to inform her about the incident and ask her to come and fetch George. Aileen immediately contacted Steve but was told by him to deal with the situation. Aileen pleaded with him to talk to George but he refused to come to school or home now he knew what was waiting for him. Truth be told, he wasn't capable of talking to George about his birth mother. Steve's response was simply to go out to the pub with his mates after work and not come home till late that evening.

Aileen rushed to the school alone and found George waiting in the headmaster's office. As soon as Aileen appeared in George's sight, he ran and wrapped his arms around her tightly and wouldn't let go. He was visibly distressed. Aileen comforted him and promised to have a proper talk with him when they got home.

They were both quiet on the way home but questions lingered in Aileen's head. *How could those kids be so cruel and where and how did they find out about Freya?*

When they got home George was sat down and Aileen carefully explained that she wasn't in fact his real mother.

"My dear! I'm so sorry that we haven't told you before. Your birth mother was called Freya and she loved you very much, but she wasn't well and wasn't able to take care of you. She passed away when you were about two..." Aileen paused as she experienced a sudden dryness in her throat. She was so cross and disheartened at Steve not being there for his own son.

On George's wee face, Aileen saw signs of hurt and disbelief as she sensed him mentally urging her to give more information. Aileen looked George right in the eye to make him understand the significance of her words and continued, "She loved you very, very much and I love you very, very much! I was married before and my husband and I were not getting along so I left that home and came to live with you and your dad. I've a son about three years older than you. His name is Alistair. He now lives in the US with his father's family," Aileen told it straight with words she hoped George would comprehend without having to reveal too much about Freya's struggle with her mental health.

George was understandably upset for hours before Aileen was finally able to soothe him and put him to bed. Aileen assured him repeatedly about how much she loved him and that she would never leave him. She waited until he fell asleep and only then she softly crept out of the room leaving the door half open in case he called for her. She went to the bathroom. She let out a sorrowful silent sigh and held both hands over her face, not able to look at her own image in the mirror. At the back of her mind, she tried to rationalise that it was the right decision not to tell George about his earlier life till that day, although in fact, it was not her decision to make, but rather Steve's. She felt responsible for him and worried that one day he would resent his father. Sooner or later George would have to deal with his past and how that would affect his life, particularly when Steve was not able to show his true feelings or talk about Freya, not even to her. She'd also had a few discussions with Steve hinting that he should be more affectionate and gentle towards George but it always ended up in an argument. She suspected that when Freya died, he shut down all his emotions because it was easier for him than having to deal with the pain and the grief. All these thoughts moved her to tears. She tightly covered her mouth with her hand, not wanting to wake up George.

Aileen massaged her temples with her fingers hoping the pressure would subdue the pain of a throbbing headache that was beginning to overcome her. She started to reflect on her life and the choices she'd made, married to a man who was unable to show his affection towards his own son. A man so much of a coward that he went to the pub with his mates and left her to deal with this incident. Her mind then turned to thinking about Alistair, whom she hadn't seen for over two years. She was tormented with regrets about not being the mother for Alistair. She felt as though she had betrayed and abandoned him.

In the days that followed, George became quieter than usual after that incident at school and also grew even more attached to Aileen. Many nights she had to stay in his room till he fell asleep. Aileen was mindful of him and more patient as she knew he needed time to digest what had been revealed to him. Understandably, all George was able to think about was finding out more about his birth mother through his father. He went over questions he prepared in his head that he would like answers to again and again but was reluctant to approach his father because of Steve's unpredictable temper.

One day after their supper, Aileen went to take out the rubbish and told them she needed to run to the shop as they were out of milk for breakfast the next morning. George took a quick peek at his father in the living room from the kitchen where he was hiding. He saw Steve sitting comfortably in an armchair holding a can of beer in his hand enjoying it while watching his favourite program on TV. George thought the right moment had come and took his chance. With his heart pounding, George tiptoed near his father. He was hopeful and thought his father would be pleased with his initiative.

"You'll never ask or talk about her as long as you live in this household. You understand!" snarled Steve in response as he saw red. He hissed and leaned forward towards George with a scowl on his face, glaring straight at him before firmly gripping his arm to show he meant business.

George quickly nodded and held back his tears. He avoided Steve's intense stare because he didn't want his disappointment and humiliation to show. It dawned on him that, based on his father's reaction, asking for a photo of his mother would not be a good idea. George had just turned seven but he'd well learned when not to push Steve's buttons further. When Aileen came back from the shop, both George and Steve acted as if nothing had happened but for the period of time that followed, George woke up easily and frequently during the nights and experienced nightmares and bed-wetting which Aileen hid from Steve worrying that likely his attitude towards it would further damage George.

As time passed, George kind of forgot about Freya and stopped asking about her. As far as he was concerned, Aileen was his mother and the only mother who cared for him. Maybe it came from some sort of self-defence mechanism in order to avoid hurt.

George learned from Aileen at a later stage that Freya had struggled with her mental health and also about the circumstances that caused her to give up on life. As much as he made an effort to feel no resentment towards his own birth mother, the pain of losing her had become deeply engraved in his heart that made him furious at her for abandoning him. For a long time, George still struggled to fathom what committing suicide really meant and the reason why his mother might have chosen not to be his mother (as he saw it).

From time to time, the thought of Freya did pop into his mind at odd times, creating an unconscious longing for her. One particular time was when he was about ten. One night when Steve was out drinking with his pals in the pub as usual, George got a fishbone stuck in his throat while eating fish pie that Aileen had made for his tea. Both Aileen and George were terrified. After a few unsuccessful attempts at trying home remedies, such as drinking a small amount of vinegar and soda or swallowing a large bite of banana, the fishbone just wouldn't move. He cried and complained about the pain and discomfort each time he swallowed.

In the end, Aileen left a note on the kitchen table for Steve and rushed to the nearest A&E with George. After they reported to the reception and were waiting for the doctor, Aileen held George in her arms comforting him. George remembered that although Aileen hugged him ever so tightly, he still cried profusely. Apart from the discomfort and just the fact they were in the hospital, he also cried for the first time missing his birth mother, for a split-second wondering if she would have taken better care of him by double-checking the fish pie for bones. As soon as that thought crossed his mind, he shrugged off the hug from Aileen and sulkily moved to a corner to sob in silence, as he felt abashed for doubting Aileen's love for him, for the first and only time.

*

"George, are you OK? You seemed a million miles away," said Aileen as she gently nudged George's arm, snapping him out of his daydream.

"Erm, I'm grand. What did Kimberly say?"

"Sarah is taking them out for a meal. The kids are excited. They asked about you," Aileen summarised her conversation.

"I'll give her and Sarah a call later this evening. I also need to confirm with Sarah her arrival time as I promised to pick her up from the train station. She insisted that she write it down on a piece of paper she left in the kitchen. I checked and checked and nowhere did I see that piece of paper! One of us is losing our mind."

George cocked an eyebrow and pulled a face. "Mum, what do you want for dinner? I'll order some takeaway. My treat, what do you fancy?" George went to the kitchen searching for takeaway menus.

After enjoying a nice meal together, George cleared the table while Aileen put the kettle on. In her head, she was contemplating whether or not to bring up another sensitive subject with George.

"Ta," said George in response to the cup of tea Aileen put on the table in front of him.

"Love. You might say it's none of my business but Sarah told me you've lost contact with Andrew," mentioned Aileen as she gently looked at George, hoping he would understand her intention was not to intrude. She just didn't want him to have the same regret one day of not seeing family members.

Not sure how to respond, George's neck and face turned red betraying his discomfort. He lowered his head and his posture shrunk, like a child sitting uncomfortably in front of a lecturing adult. Knowing her good intentions, he still felt as if Sarah had gone behind his back by talking to Aileen.

"After all, Andrew is your cousin. Should I invite you all over for dinner?" suggested Aileen, her eyes lighting up at her own initiative.

"No. Oh. No need," without hesitation, George quickly declined. "Sarah has invited him over a few times but he always said he was busy so let's put it on ice for now."

"OK. As you wish. Remember, it's too late for your father but not too late for you," Aileen pointed out.

With those words ringing in his head, George said his goodbyes and left. On the bus home, he began to mull over whether or not he should have a last try with Andrew. It truly puzzled him that their relationship had gone downhill after their first contact in 2019, which drew him into a gloomy mood. Without any warning, George burped and once he realised where he was, he made a fake cough as a disguise. He embarrassedly had a quick peep around hoping no one had been disturbed by the odour coming out of his stomach. He massaged his chest at the sensation of heartburn, puzzling over the source of his discomfort; was it caused by the spicy food he'd just had or the discussion Aileen had brought up about Andrew?

After George left, while clearing away the rubbish and takeaway containers, Aileen had her own doubts and regrets as she reflected on her first marriage to Alistair's father, Ken Park, in 1958 as well as her second marriage to George's father, Steve, eight years later.

Chapter 3 – 1958

Mr and Mrs Park Senior were successful hotel owners in Edinburgh and their son Ken worked for them.

One day Ken was visiting one of the hotels owned by his parents with a roofer to discuss how to repair a leak caused by recent heavy storms. There he bumped into Aileen, who was working as a chambermaid. After that initial meeting, Ken started to visit that particular hotel more frequently with the excuse of overseeing the work on the roof. Secretly he was there to see Aileen.

Ken was about five years older than Aileen. He was handsome, sophisticated, well-educated and with good manners, unlike the other boys Aileen had associated with before. Aileen was beautiful and fearless, a girl who spoke her mind, despite being petite, which attracted Ken. Aileen came from a humble background and had dropped out of school so she was fascinated with the exclusive places Ken started taking her to, fancy restaurants, dance halls, all places she'd never dreamt of going.

In the beginning, Aileen didn't take it seriously, just thought it was fun to go out with the owner's son who treated her so well. At first, they saw each other secretly but as their relationship grew and they saw more of each other, rumours and gossip started to circulate and soon reached Mr and Mrs Park Senior.

"You should *not* be dating one of the staff members! Others would see it as being unprofessional," Ken's father opined, hoping it was no more than just a fling and that his son would come to his senses. Mr Park Senior was as tactful as he could be and hid his disapproval well, not wanting to push Ken into a corner. At the time Ken dutifully nodded in agreement to please his father, though he had no intention whatsoever of breaking off the relationship with Aileen.

Ken's mother, meanwhile, was more vocal about her dislike of Aileen. Mrs Park Senior was horrified and furious when she found out about the affair happening under her nose. She viewed Aileen as simple, common and uneducated. She expected Ken to meet someone better, someone who would fit well among their own aspiring social and financial circle, someone who appreciated the finer things in life and had an understanding of politics and world affairs. Not a school dropout and certainly not a chambermaid.

After the discussion with his father and his mother openly criticising Aileen, Ken helped Aileen find a job elsewhere. He worked out it was best to get her out of his parents' sight and also hoped to avoid any further gossip and smirking remarks from the other workers.

Following their plan, Aileen left the hotel for another job and Ken acted as though he was not bothered by it and never mentioned her at all. Mrs Park Senior's intuition on the other hand told her that it wouldn't be that straightforward and she sensed that she had to act quickly. She started organising dinner parties in their house inviting their friends to bring their daughters, granddaughters or nieces along. Ken knew immediately that his mother was cooking up something. Many times he would either not show up or make a disappearance mid-dinner without informing anyone, which caused many arguments in the Park house. The whole charade ended when one day Ken came back and announced that Aileen was expecting and she had accepted when he'd asked for her hand in marriage.

After they got married, Ken and Aileen lived in a flat in one of the hotels family Park owned and, worse yet, Ken's parents lived in the penthouse right above them. At that time Ken was still working for his parents and didn't have his own money.

Aileen struggled to fit into her new role as the young Mrs Park as she was consistently criticised and received patronising and degrading comments from her mother-in-law about her lack of knowledge in high society interactions and gatherings. She was also pressured into working in the office which she was not educated or trained for. She felt as if her soul was being chipped away bit by bit.

Ken saw Aileen was drowning in her new role and life so he tried his best to support her but he was mostly away busy working for the family business. He was very conflicted because on the one hand, he witnessed Aileen being talked down to and looked down on by his mother but on the other hand he didn't have the courage to challenge his own mother. He felt obliged to obey his mother; after all his parents still controlled the whole business and his finances. He told Aileen that they had to play their cards right and later, once he got hold of the business, things would change for the better. He begged Aileen to be patient and gave her a vague promise that they could move out once the baby was born.

What disappointed Aileen the most was that with Ken's salary, they could definitely have afforded to find a place of their own but not to the standards Ken was expected. Living in the same building as his parents had its perks with a cleaner, cooks and most importantly it was rent-free. Knowing her husband well, she knew he wouldn't be able to let go of living in an affluent part of town; it complemented his image and ego, not to mention the comfort he was accustomed to.

After baby Alistair was born, Aileen stopped working in order to care for him and her nightmare only worsened. She was heartbroken to learn that Ken had no real intention of moving out like he'd promised time and again. She was so isolated and felt that she had lost her own voice and was trapped in a gilded cage. Each day she lived in fear as each time Alistair cried she would receive cutting remarks from Mrs Park Senior. In her mother-in-law's point of view, children were to be seen and not heard. Each time Alistair cried, Aileen could imagine her mother-in-law rolling her eyes thinking that Aileen wasn't a good mother.

When Alistair turned one Aileen would often bring him to her parents' place and leave him there with them the whole afternoon. She would then stroll to the park nearby and just sit in a swing watching and staring at people passing by. It was her me-time, when she could just forget who she was and what was expected of her.

One day after she dropped off Alistair at her parents', on her way to the park Aileen bumped into Scot, a schoolmate she used to fancy. He had gone to the same school as her. Although three years her senior, he had been required to redo a year twice, so they ended up in the same school year but in different classes, before they both dropped out of high school. Scot was one of the favourites among the girls in school with his blond hair, good looks and long legs. The girls used to joke about Scot's Hollywood jawline. So it was flattering for Aileen when Scot remembered and approached her.

While walking together to the park Aileen kept her head down and it was mostly Scot who initiated the conversation. Seeing the reflection of the sunshine on his golden hair when he carelessly skipped along kicking the leaves Aileen felt perplexed but happy. She discovered a smile on her face when she sensed Scot was eager to please her. During their encounter, Aileen learned that Scot was unemployed and was only able to find odd jobs here and there. He did most of the talking and Aileen answered simply yes or no to questions. To break the awkward silence and break out of the one-way conversation, an impulsive idea suddenly entered Scot's mind. He started walking backwards and waved at Aileen at the same time, playing the fool for her.

"You're so silly!" Aileen giggled and her guard melted.

Laughing together, they sat down on a bench in the park. The ice was finally broken and they found they had no shortage of topics for their chats once they got started. They asked each other about what had happened to other schoolmates and expressed their common hate for their former teachers. Aileen sensed she was able to breathe when she was around Scot. She laughed at his silly jokes and felt at ease in his company because she didn't need to pretend or worry about making mistakes.

At that time, she felt as though Scot was heaven-sent. With him, there was no complicated etiquette to follow and she didn't need to be mindful of how she spoke or used words.

Without noticing it, the smiles lingered on her face for days after meeting Scot. She even found her mother-in-law's criticisms somewhat tolerable and at times hilarious which aggravated Mrs Park Senior beyond the limit of her patience. One day, Mrs Park disparagingly called out Aileen for being distracted while feeding Alistair. Aileen was holding the bottle with her hand frozen in the air while her mind was preoccupied with thinking about Scot and his jokes.

Aileen made up excuses to visit her parents with Alistair more regularly when her parents were able to look after him, as she sought every opportunity to see Scot. Scot was skint so they often met in the park when the weather permitted. A few times Scot would show Aileen petty thefts he'd stolen from various stores. Other times he would also bring her shoplifted make-up and even small toys for Alistair which she thought was sweet at first. However, as time went on Aileen became uncomfortable when he came with more substantial items he had snatched from shops. She told him to stop before getting caught but he just brushed it off, bragging how skilful and untouchable he was. It was his way to impress her, the only way he knew.

Aileen was astonished when one day Scot brought with him a sizeable ball-shaped watermelon he'd stolen. Her mouth opened and shut wordlessly a few times. Staring at him in disbelief as he carried it hilariously around with both hands she finally asked, "How did you even manage to hide a watermelon inside your jacket and walk out of the store without anyone noticing?"

Scot shrugged his shoulders and smirked, proud.

They kicked the watermelon around like a football and as it cracked, the flesh of the melon scattered everywhere, which made them laugh their heads off.

An older man nearby saw the mess they'd made and started yelling at them. Scot grabbed hold of Aileen's hand and they ran away from the park till they were both out of breath. In that exact moment, Aileen felt free and alive. She was not a wife, not a mother, not a daughter-in-law, she was just Aileen.

"Want to come? I know a place where we can go," asked Scot. "Don't worry, we don't need to do anything you don't want to," Scot reassured her when he glimpsed doubt on Aileen's face. Aileen avoided eye contact with

Scot but quietly followed him. That day their affair started.

Aileen regretted at once the first time they slept together in a filthy apartment Scot had borrowed from his friend for an hour. She wanted to stop seeing him but at the same time, a voice inside was asking her why she should even bother to care. Her in-laws thought nothing of her, so she wanted to do something even worse than what they expected, just to shock them. As the affair went on Aileen enjoyed it less and less, particularly when Scot became overly possessive. She didn't know how to end things and secretly hoped something or someone would do it for her.

After Aileen's increasingly suspicious disappearances, Ken was instructed by his mother to visit his in-laws unannounced to investigate and, sure enough, Aileen wasn't at her parents'. He brought Alistair home, waiting for Aileen. She eventually came home and without much hesitation confessed to Ken about the affair when he asked her what she'd been doing. She was so at ease admitting it, it was almost like she was expecting to be caught.

Surprisingly, Mrs Park Senior didn't say anything to Aileen. She never bothered to make any eye contact with her again. Alistair was taken away from Aileen to be looked after by a nanny. Mrs Park Senior totally blindsided Aileen and swiftly ordered staff to gather Aileen's belongings and sent them back to her parents. Aileen swore she found a hint of a snigger in her mother-in-law while she was busy ordering everyone around.

Most importantly, Mrs Park Senior said to her son in front of Aileen that she insisted and demanded they get divorced.

After Aileen moved back to her parents, Mrs Park Senior forbade her to see Alistair at all. The situation only improved once Ken intervened. Aileen was forever grateful to Ken for standing up for her, for once. She was then able to spend time with Alistair when he'd been dropped off at her parents' place, but those times had to be specifically arranged and strictly monitored.

Aileen tortured herself for not being able to see her son as often and freely as she would have liked. She was facing the possibility of losing custody once the divorce happened. It broke her heart knowing that she wasn't the one who bathed him or put him to bed, fed him or comfort him when he was upset.

To make the situation worse, she found out she was pregnant without knowing who the father was. Her fear was that if it turned out to be Scot's there was no way he would be able to support them. She knew that because he could hardly support himself. Scot had also disappeared after she moved back to her parents knowing the trouble he had caused. Aileen figured asking him for help was out of the question. But then if Ken was the father the baby could be taken away from her as well.

The thought of an abortion did enter Aileen's mind but was quickly dismissed and she blamed her wicked mind for even considering it, especially since she knew it was illegal at that time. She just didn't know where or who to turn to. She kept asking herself whether and how she would be able to raise the child on her own. She kept the pregnancy a secret even from her parents. Without a doubt, they would not have supported her because they too blamed her for the affair and ruining her marriage.

While living with her parents she was also burdened with financial stress. She needed to make a living to pay rent to them and support herself. With her previous work experience, she was soon able to get a job as a cleaner in a bar that also had a few B&B rooms above it. She was over the moon to be able to earn some money. However, it all turned out to be too much for her at once and with all the stress and tormented feelings of guilt, regret, shame and hopelessness, she suffered a miscarriage. She cried for days when she was alone in her room for the pain of losing her baby and missing Alistair.

One solace was her work; it kept her busy. She was good at the work and appreciated by the owner. After a while, she started putting in extra hours collecting empty glasses in the bar as well. A far-fetched dream she had was that if only she could save some money maybe she could afford to have a small place of her own where she could raise Alistair in the future.

As the job was so important for Aileen she worked extra hard and at times went above and beyond to clean every guest room to a high level. Her effort was soon recognised by the owner and also by customers because of her pleasant, cheerful nature. The owner offered her a room and she was overjoyed that she was able to move out of her parents and gain back her independence. She worked even harder because the work was more significant to her than making money; it was also a place where she could forget about her troubled private life.

Aileen did not recall when but she started to notice a customer who would come in after work hours and sit quietly drinking his pints in a corner by himself, not interacting with other customers. He dragged his feet when he walked and his posture sagged with defeat written on his face like he was carrying all the troubles of the world on his shoulders. She didn't think much of it at first but soon she was drawn to him. *Poor soul. What could be that bad? I thought I was the one who had enough sorrows for both of us.* She told herself that she would talk to him the next time she saw him, which she did the next day.

"Hi! Gosh, the storms and the winds last night were horrendous," said Aileen, rubbing her arms as if a cold wind had just entered the bar.

The customer raised his head and with an empty stare, he gazed at this woman in front of him. He was uncertain if she was even speaking to him. She had such an aura of scintillating energy that frightened him. He opened his mouth but he found himself tongue-tied. He was miles away, drowning in his own thoughts and miseries. He put his head down again.

"Sorry, didn't mean to disturb you. By the way, my name is Aileen and I work here. Another one?" Aileen pointed at the customer's empty glass and then picked it up and put it in a tray. "You should try our homemade steak pie!" Aileen had observed him for a few days and he looked gaunt with sunken cheeks; she assumed he hadn't had a good meal for some while.

The customer lifted his head up from his pint and was taken aback at the introduction made by Aileen. *Why would someone talk to me?*

"And you are?"

"Erm. I'm Steve." The customer introduced himself with a nod.

Aileen had no doubts in her mind that she saw a smile hidden somewhere in his stony facial expression.

After the first interaction, they would have short conversations each time they saw each other in the bar. A few weeks passed by and Steve's icy demeanour began to thaw but he remained a closed book not revealing much about himself. Aileen, on the other hand, was open about her situation and often spoke about her longing for her son.

"Would you like to visit Portobello beach one day when you're not working? I'm sure we both need a break," nervously asked Steve, while avoiding eye contact. He also lowered his voice because he didn't want others in the bar to hear.

Aileen appreciated his gesture and thought it must have taken him a lot of courage to ask the question in a way that implied it wasn't a 'date' because he knew well that Aileen was still in the middle of her divorce procedure at that time.

A week or so later they went to Portobello beach and walked along the promenade enjoying the sun and ice cream.

"Anything the matter?" Aileen asked, licking around the cone while the ice cream was melting. "You seem extremely quiet."

"I want to tell you something…" Steve began but trailed off, unsure how to continue his sentence.

"What is it? Can't be that bad!" replied Aileen as she first slowed down then stopped walking altogether. She studied Steve from the corner of her eye, trying to figure out what could be so difficult for him to tell her.

"I…"

"Steve, you don't need to tell me anything if you don't want to." *Maybe it's better I don't know?* Out of nowhere a knot of anxiety grew in her stomach.

"I want to. I… I don't have anyone to talk to. Just give me a minute," Steve pleaded. Looking out at the sea, breathing quickly in and out, for a moment he felt the tightness in his chest was about to explode. One thought that kept ringing in his head was his worry that she would think less of him after she knew about his story.

Standing next to Steve, Aileen didn't say anything. She sensed it was something extremely personal. She could see that he was struggling with whatever emotion was inside. She simply placed a hand on his back.

Once Steve had calmed down and overcome the first hesitation he finally told Aileen about his situation, Freya and George. At times he jumped back and forth in his story-telling and Aileen had to ask him to repeat or clarify so that she could understand.

Eventually, the story ended and they both stopped talking. Aileen turned her head to one side to avoid eye contact with Steve so as not to make him uncomfortable. She was truly saddened by what happened to Steve and the depth of his hurt. What Steve told her was beyond what she was able to imagine. She was astonished to learn that he had been carrying so many wounds inside him for so long and had no one to talk to. His parents had passed away years ago and he was estranged from his brother. He'd lost his wife to suicide not long ago and his boy had been put into foster care. *How was it possible for a man to bear so much loss and sorrow?*

That day was the day they grew closer, though they still remained at the level of friends at that point.

A few days later Steve came by the bar and told Aileen that he was allowed to take George from his temporary foster home to a park for a few hours and asked if she would like to meet them there.

Aileen was excited and apprehensive about meeting George for the first time and wanted to make a good impression. She was worried for nothing because as soon as she saw him looking back at her, a wee adorable face with freckles, their eyes locked and her heart melted. She leaned forward to say hello and give him a cuddly toy. George giggled and grabbed the toy in one hand and held tightly to two of her fingers with the other for a good while.

"George, c'mon, say hello to Aileen." Steve picked up George from his pushchair and handed him over to Aileen.

As soon as she held him in her arms, much to her surprise, she welled up. Steve understood she was missing her own son.

Aileen and Steve started spending more time with each other outside the bar where she worked and their feelings towards each other slowly blossomed. They were not intimate at that time, something Aileen insisted on and which Steve respected. He saw a future with her and he particularly appreciated how George and her were fond of each other.

The marriage of Ken and Aileen came to an official end with a divorce just before the end of 1965. At that time, a woman in her status didn't have too much of a choice or voice. Aileen didn't challenge the decision about the custody of Alistair being awarded to Ken because she was the one who'd had the affair that had led to the breakdown of their marriage.

With the divorce finalised, one consolation was that Aileen was given rights by the court to spend a certain amount of time with Alistair. Alistair would be dropped off at Aileen's parents because she felt inadequate having him in her little room above the pub.

Aileen was taken aback when she learned Ken had remarried very quickly after the divorce. In her mind, the ink on their divorce paper wasn't even dry. But then she reasoned with herself that she had no right to be bitter or judgemental. She was emotionally involved with Steve as well. Aileen started getting serious with Steve and they were married within a year of her divorce.

Did they genuinely love each other or did they both marry only for convenience and necessity? The question was in everyone's minds, including Steve and Aileen's, when they walked down the aisle. One thing was for sure though, they knew they were marrying for the right reason because they wanted to mend two broken hearts and could support each other so that they were able to provide a safe and stable home for George. After they got married, social services re-evaluated Steve's case and George was eventually able to come home to stay with him and Aileen, first on a temporary trial basis and then permanently.

After she got remarried, she drew a line and turned her back on her past. She wanted to prove to herself and anyone who doubted her that she was worthy and decent. She was a good wife to Steve and a devoted mother to George; it was her way of paying her dues for her previous mistakes.

Aileen still saw Alistair but it became more cumbersome because Steve made it clear to her that he didn't want to know anything about him and wasn't that keen on her seeing him too often. He did not forbid those meetings, but he made Aileen understand that he would turn a blind eye to it as long as he was not aware of the details and it didn't inconvenience his life. He asked that her priority now be him and George.

Another contributing factor making it difficult for Aileen to see Alistair was the attitude of Ken's new wife. The new young Mrs Park didn't want Aileen to be any part of their lives, unless obligated by law, even less than

Aileen's ex-mother-in-law. She didn't want Alistair spending too much time with Aileen because she thought it could be a bad influence.

In order to be able to see more of Alistair, when time allowed, Aileen would hide outside the entrance of school watching Alistair coming out to be picked up by his new mum. It broke her heart that she wasn't the one who greeted little Alistair when he first came out from the school.

Aileen went through a period of deep despondency then, not that Steve noticed or cared to ask. Life went on. She poured all her love into George and cared for him as her own. She had a busy life taking care of her new family, especially with such a demanding husband.

Chapter 4 – 2019

"Dad, do you think this guy could be your cousin?" Kimberly stayed on the line after the family called to wish George a happy birthday.

"What? Who?" George was caught off guard by the question.

"You know, your cousin, Andrew. Let me forward you a photo and the details of him I found on his Facebook profile. Have a look and phone me back!" she excitedly instructed her father.

After seeing the photo and the profile details George called Kimberly back straight away, now both bewildered and surprised.

"What brought it up? How did you find him?" he asked.

"I meant to tell you but with the kids just recovering from stomach bugs I totally forgot about it until today. About ten days ago, just by chance, I went through my 'People You May Know' list on Facebook and his profile was one of them. I assume it was because he has the same last name as ours, Hughes. I can never figure it out either, how those people are suggested to you, truth be told."

"You know me. I know nothing about social media and can't be bothered with it either. For me, those apps are a world totally beyond my comprehension."

They both laughed.

"Have you ever met him?"

"I've heard of him but never met him though, nor his father. I believe his father and your granddad fell out when they were younger and never got back in contact," explained George, scratching his itchy nose.

There were two topics Steve had never talked about ever since George was little; Freya, his first wife and Neil, his brother. George did hear bits and pieces through Aileen about why the two brothers' falling out happened but as time went by, he kind of forgot about it, in particular after he got married and had a family of his own and now he was a granddad himself.

"Dad, are you still there?" queried Kimberly, realizing George had gone quiet for a bit.

George was brought back to their conversation. "Aye, I'm here, I'm here! It's not that we can ask Granddad now he's in the care home, and with the stage of his dementia I'm sure he can't remember much," said George, sounding deflated.

"Andrew owns a successful trendy interior design firm helping exclusive clients with house renovation work. From the photos showing the work he's done, I worked out they don't come cheap! Wait though, there's another interesting thing mentioned in his profile. A novel was mentioned there, so I went on Amazon and found out more. I read the blurb and placed an order right away. I just finished reading it."

"Andrew wrote a novel?"

"No. An author named Tom Gibbs wrote a fiction novel apparently based on Andrew's life!" Kimberly clarified.

"Really, how fascinating! What happened in his life?" Now George was intrigued.

"All kinds of things! In the book, the main character's dad had a dispute with his brother after their mother died. The dad went to New Zealand and never returned when the main character was very young so he was raised single-handedly by his mother. Then there was a tragedy about his son later on. There's a lot of stuff about grief and letting go of regrets. Oh and there's something about the main character being gay as well," summarised Kimberly.

George was quiet, absorbing all the information Kimberly had just told him.

"I thought it was very touching. And it made me think about a rare occasion when Granddad complained to me once about his dispute with his brother. If I remember it correctly, it was about the inheritance after their mother died so that fits with what's in the book. I know reading fiction is not your thing though. I will send it to Mum tomorrow. I won't tell you more about it in case you do fancy having a go!" she teased.

"Erm, I'm pretty sure your mum would love to read it. I'll talk to your Nan and see if she can tell me more," replied George, tactfully declining the suggestion about him reading the novel himself.

"OK! Bye, Dad. Tell Mum I'll call her later once I've put the kids to bed. I better go now, they're screaming their lungs out for me to read their bedtime stories!" said Kimberly, mimicking a childish scream.

The book arrived two days after their conversation and Sarah read it with intense interest. She was moved a few times when reading about the main character's son's death in a car accident. The main character had to fly over to the US to take care of his son's funeral. The heart-breaking scenario where he had to choose a coffin for his son and what clothes to wear was also very emotional, particularly for Sarah now she was a mother and a grandmother. She shuddered at the thought of losing Kimberly or her children. Her thoughts went out to Andrew whom she'd never met knowing how tough it must have been for him to lose a child to a car accident and then to have to arrange the funeral.

A few days after Kimberly's call, George went over to see Aileen and told her about Andrew and the book based on what he'd learned from Kimberly and Sarah.

From what was written in the book and what Aileen remembered they came to some conclusions.

George's father, Steve, had a brother, Neil. When Steve and Neil were little, their father bought a corner shop in Stockbridge, which the family ran for years, even after their father had passed away when the two boys were in their early teens. Apparently, numerous times Steve was blamed for being late settling bills with suppliers and for money disappearing from the till after he had been minding the shop. Then, when the boys' mother died a few years later, she gave some money to

Steve but left the corner shop to Neil even though Steve was the eldest.

"I mean; you could say a lot about my father but I'm surprised to hear that he was accused of stealing from his own family! That must have been terrible for him," opined George, shaking his head.

"It happened when he was in his late teens or early twenties and I met him when he was in his early thirties. I can't imagine your father being reckless with money. We always paid our bills on time! He never spoke much about his childhood or his family. He did tell me once that he blamed his mother for favouring his brother, which he never forgave her for. He moved out from their family home and cut any contact with his brother," said Aileen with a sigh.

After his visit to Aileen, George took time to digest it all for a few days then called Kimberly and asked her to get in contact with Andrew on Facebook.

"Dad, listen, I messaged Andrew and he confirmed he's your cousin. He was surprised but also kind of thrilled that I found him! He gave me his phone number and asked you to phone him," reported Kimberly to George after her initial exchange with Andrew.

"Cheers. Let me have a think about it," mumbled George.

George sat silently on the living room sofa after the call with Kimberly. He bit his lip and his posture froze awkwardly. He stared at the piece of paper where he'd written down the phone number.

"You have to make that call! You've nothing to lose and what happened between your dads was long ago, it's water under the bridge now! You're fifty-six, how much longer are you going to wait?" asked Sarah incredulously as she walked into the living room from the kitchen to hand a cup of tea to George.

George looked at her with mixed emotions running all over his face.

Sitting across from George and looking at him, Sarah had to admit it couldn't be easy to suddenly talk to one's cousin whom one had never met. She knew her husband well enough to know that at times like this he needed some sort of encouragement and then should be left alone to make his own choice.

"I'll go out to the shop now to give you some peace and quiet to talk to Andrew. What about Mexican for tea?" proposed Sarah as she rose from the sofa. She gave George a smile and a tap on his shoulder that suggested she appreciated him being apprehensive about making that call.

George smiled back and nodded but neither of them was sure whether he was agreeing to her suggestion about the dinner or that he would call Andrew.

Phew, he exhaled a breath he didn't know he'd been holding when he saw Sarah close the door behind her on her way to the shop.

George collected his thoughts for a few moments before he walked to the kitchen, opened a cabinet and reached for a bottle of whisky and poured himself a sizeable glass. *I need something strong.* Only once in a blue moon would he enjoy the occasional glass of wine with food during festival celebrations. He was never a big drinker, never mind touching hard spirits. He liked his sugary carbonated drinks and could drink a large bottle in one go if he was in the mood. Whisky, however, was a rarity for him. George took a huge gulp and coughed instantly as he drank it too fast and it went down the wrong way. After a few moments, he calmed down. He cleared his throat, put on his reading glasses and stared at his phone for a moment before he anxiously dialled the number.

The two cousins talked for the first time and astonishingly the conversation went well, flowing quite smoothly without much awkwardness. After all, the fireworks between their fathers were long gone and forgotten. As far as George and Andrew both saw it, the dispute between their fathers had nothing to do with them. They therefore agreed to meet up in a café the following day, a Saturday, in Leith to talk more.

"Aye, we should hold an umbrella or wear a blue scarf or something so we can recognise each other," suggested George with a mock serious tone in his voice and they both burst into laughter before they hung up.

After the call, George felt ecstatic and he paced around the kitchen and wasn't able to sit down. He called Kimberly and Aileen right away and told them about the conversation and the arranged meet-up with Andrew and they were both really pleased for him.

"See, it wasn't that bad, was it?" said Sarah with twinkling eyes as she patted George's back affectionately. George had filled her in about the call as soon as she got back from the shop.

Chapter 5 – 2019

Andrew arrived at the café holding an umbrella in his hand as a joke. He was early. He opened the door and stepped inside, turning his head around for a quick glance over the place. As it was just after ten, there weren't many people. He didn't recognise anybody that could be George. He closed the door and waited outside. In a way, he was relieved to be there before George because he cherished the moment of arriving first and being alone to digest the idea of meeting up with his cousin for the first time. In reality, he'd been afflicted with unsettling thoughts in his head about the outcome of this meeting ever since Kimberly first contacted him on Facebook.

Looking at the café window he noticed a promotional display of Christmas coffees. He then turned to have a good look at the street and, watching cars and people passing by, he realised that the Christmas decorations were already up. *So early! It's only the beginning of November.*

Andrew's mind started wandering and he recognised he was feeling unsettled about today's meeting with George. *What to expect and what was expected of him?* Before Kimberly contacted him, he didn't think he had any other close family members. He had cousins from his mother's sister, Aunt Betty, whose family had emigrated to Canada when Andrew was young. Ever since the death of his mother and Aunt Betty, the contact with her children had noticeably cooled off. Andrew was still friends with them on Facebook but they only contacted each other with seasonal and birthday greetings. So for Andrew, he'd been a real loner till Kimberly reached out to him. It was such a revelation for him to discover he had other relatives out there looking for him.

A car horn blared as someone ran through a red light. Andrew watched the incident unfold in front of him and then went back to his thoughts. He'd lost Nathan, his son, when he was nineteen. Nathan had died just a few months before turning twenty. *How old would Nathan be today, thirty-two?* Andrew closed his eyes for a moment and his heart ached. Though it was less painful to think about Nathan, so many years after his death, the sorrow remained. He then reflected on his childhood, with his mother, Hilary, who'd died nine years ago. Then his thoughts turned to his father, Neil Hughes, who'd gone to New Zealand to work on a sheep farm. At first, Neil sent letters and money home but then the contact ceased. When Andrew became old enough, he did ask his mother why she didn't try to contact him and was told that any letters she sent were returned unopened with his name and address crossed out on the envelope.

Andrew often wondered how his mother had agreed for his father to travel to a place so far away. He couldn't imagine how hard the discussions had been before his father's departure. He also thought that it must have been heartbreaking for his mother to accept her fate when he ceased all contact. Andrew tried many times to reason in his head about the circumstances that caused his father to leave and his decision not to keep in contact or to return. In Andrew's head, he felt strongly that it was somehow his fault that his father had left them. But what had he done that caused his father to abandon them? It was a question that echoed in his head over and over again without him being able to find a satisfying answer.

For many years he was upset about the shame and mystery of his absent father. In the seventies, growing up in a single-parent family wasn't easy for his mum, nor for Andrew. Andrew was teased numerous times at school for not having a father. Being a single mother, Hilary, although loving and caring, had had to make rational and practical decisions rather than emotional ones because bills had to be paid and food needed to be put on the table. As he grew older he held back from asking about his dad mainly because his mother was so dejected when speaking about him. In order not to upset his mother further, he stopped even mentioning him but his father was never far from his mind, whether missing him, hating him, being angry with him or being disappointed with him.

Where is he now? Is he still alive? Did he have another family? Did he ever think about my mum and me? Those were the questions ringing in Andrew's head when growing up. Andrew recalled in his mind that he'd even imagined bumping into his father on the street and how he would tell him off.

Andrew's irritation suddenly grew and he felt blood rushing angrily to his head. Both his face and fists tightened. He felt light-headed and forced himself to release his fists and leaned against the wall with one hand to regain his balance. He let out a deep breath and shook his head, wondering why his father had come to his mind so intrusively. *It must be because I'm meeting up with George*, he reasoned. It bothered him that he was still emotionally vulnerable when thinking about his father.

"Andrew!" shouted a man waving an umbrella in his hand from a distance.

They had never met before but as soon as Andrew saw him somehow in his mind he registered it was surely George.

They both chuckled as Andrew waved his in return.

"Wait a second!" said George breathlessly as he approached and held a hand to his chest, making it clear that he needed a few moments to compose himself.

"Are you all right?" enquired Andrew.

George nodded. He stretched out his arm for a handshake once he'd caught his breath. After he got hold of Andrew's hand he pulled him forwards and gave him a heartfelt hug. "For God's sake, not just a handshake!" George exclaimed.

Unexpectedly, Andrew felt a lump in his throat. He found himself tongue-tied at that moment because he would never have imagined meeting his cousin one day and being greeted so warmly by him.

George then let go of the hug. "Cuz, how are you? Sorry, I'm a bit late. I'm usually on time if not too early.

The bus was re-routed due to the tram works in this area. I got off one stop earlier. Because of the traffic, the bus stood still for a good fifteen minutes!" George drew a breath before he continued, "I tried to walk as quickly as I could. You see my bad knees mean I can't walk too fast or for too long of a stretch these days. But if I don't walk enough then it's not good either! It's rather a catch-22 situation," explained George in hyper-tempo.

"Don't worry about it! Who cares about a few minutes, we waited more than fifty years to meet up," Andrew pointed out.

George nodded happily in agreement.

Unconsciously, both cousins glanced over at each other and simultaneously offered a polite smile.

"How are you keeping anyway? How old are you now?" asked George with great interest.

"OK, thanks. I can't complain. You're fifty-six, right? I'll be fifty-two in a few months. We're getting old, but, touch wood, I still have my hair!" Andrew joked and with his fist, he knocked gently at the right side of his temple twice.

They both laughed.

"Yes, two old farts," joked George, trying his best to hide his belly without realising it only to attract more attention to it. He patted Andrew's back. "Let's go in for a drink. It's getting chilly." He opened the door and gestured with his hand to invite Andrew to enter first.

"Cheers." Andrew grinned as he walked in. He opened his mouth, wanting to say something witty back like *No, thanks. Speak for yourself,* referring to the remark about being 'Two Old Farts'. At the last moment, he changed his mind because he didn't feel he knew George well enough to judge whether or not he would be offended by such a comment.

George insisted on buying drinks for them both because he was the oldest.

They sat down and at first the conversation started well with how amazed they both were they had never crossed paths though they lived in the same city. After that, the conversation kind of dried up because neither knew what to say next. After all, they were in fact two strangers, so to speak.

It was easier to talk over the phone. The same thought entered both cousins' minds.

So they were silent. They avoided looking at each other. One looked at the coffee cup and kept stirring the teaspoon around. The other studied the menu on the wall over his shoulder.

After a few more awkward moments, George reinitiated the conversation. "So you said you live in the Haymarket area?" George turned his head to look directly at Andrew.

"Well, actually in the West End because—"

"Oh, so in the posh area of Edinburgh then!" George jumped in to finish the sentence with his own idea of things.

"Hmm…" Andrew jokingly rolled his eyes and acted like he was offended. "That is exactly why I tell people that I live in the Haymarket area. For whatever reason beyond my understanding, when The West End is mentioned occasionally people react strangely, just like you did!" Andrew emphasised, visibly uncomfortable.

"Oh. I didn't mean anything by it. It was just a flippant remark," explained George. He did not understand why Andrew would make such a big deal out of it.

"No worries."

"But I could imagine you living a posh life. You're so nicely dressed with your perfect trouser creases. I bet you never buy reduced-price items in the supermarket!" George teased and gave a sheepish grin.

Andrew's smile vanished and his mouth fell open for a moment in surprise. Andrew felt uncomfortable not knowing George's intention with his jokes, whether they were meant to be fun banter or malicious. A sudden random unrelated thought came to Andrew for no reason about the TV show Keeping Up Appearances where the main character Hyacinth loved to brag about her sister Violet who drove a Mercedes, lived in a big house with a huge garden with enough room for a pony. Imagine what outrageous thing George would say if he were to make a similar joke about his penthouse flat with a terrace enough room for a sauna and jacuzzi and so on.

Why does he look miffed? Did I say something offensive? George was puzzled why Andrew's mood had gone stale.

"I work like everyone else and I do like to find bargains," said Andrew with a hint of irritation in his voice, somewhat bewildered. As soon as the words left his mouth the question crossed his mind of why he should even need to justify himself to George!

"Hey, hope you're not offended by what I said. About reduced-price items, my wife is always embarrassed that I would go to the supermarket early and wander around just to get them in time. Have to tell you something funny though!" George tried to lighten the atmosphere by telling a joke.

Andrew's facial expression relaxed somewhat but he still kept his mental guard up.

"My old man was even worse than me! A few years ago we went out food shopping together and he lost his patience waiting for a staff member to mark down the reduced-price items in the fruit and veg section. My father approached him, looked him right in the eye and unashamedly enquired whether he wouldn't mind marking the meat section first because we had a bus to catch!" George burst into laughter while putting a hand to his forehead to show his astonishment.

"Oh, that is cheeky! What did the staff member say?" Andrew was half amused and half shocked by what he was hearing.

"The guy didn't say anything at all. He tilted his head back, gave a blank stare to my father and turned his head back and continued marking the items in front of him. I had to drag my father away from there. Even I felt embarrassed for him. Knowing my father well he would have had no problem making unpleasant remarks to the poor guy."

Simultaneously they both cracked up and after that, they became quiet again. One stared at the wall and the other looked at the people around the cafe. Both were preoccupied with trying to come up with the next topic.

"So, how is your father doing?" asked Andrew eventually.

"We visit him regularly and only on rare occasions is he able to briefly acknowledge us. To be honest, he's not getting better that is for sure. He is in the advanced stages of his dementia."

"That must be a difficult decision to make, putting him in a care home, particularly for your mum, I imagine?"

"Yes, but difficult was only half of the story. He really lost his marbles and became more than a handful, to say the least. Before placing him in a care home, numerous times my mum would come home and find him butt naked and wouldn't put any clothes on when confronted," revealed George pulling a face. "My mum also found dirty plates in the kitchen cupboard blaming the dishwasher but then discovered it was my father who hid them, for whatever reason."

"Sorry to hear that. It must've been hard for her either way..." Andrew reflected with a pause for a moment. "Maybe I should visit him sometime. Only if it's possible, of course!" he added on a whim.

"Aye, that would be nice. Unfortunately, he won't know who you are," warned George.

Andrew nodded in understanding.

"Anyway, Kimberly showed me your business website. Impressive what you do. I work for the Royal Mail and my wife Sarah is a librarian."

"Oh, cheers," replied Andrew, not knowing what else to add.

"Before I forget, what is it about the book based on your life? How did you even get to know the author? Are you a celebrity or something?" quizzed George showing his interest and trying to keep the conversation alive. He was mighty impressed with himself that he'd found a talking point.

"Oh… it was really a fiction and was only partially based on my life. Why would you assume that about being a celebrity?" asked Andrew, taken aback by George's unfounded claim about him somehow being famous.

"I just thought only famous people would appear in novels!" George explained.

"I'm nobody!" declared Andrew with a laugh.

"So, how did it start then?"

"The author's name is Tom Gibbs. He was one of my clients. A few years ago he hired me to redo his kitchen and bathroom. He liked what I'd done and we got on well and became good friends," Andrew explained. "He had so far written two novels. The first one was based on his own life being brought up by his grandparents under difficult circumstances."

George nodded, waiting to hear more.

"One time when we were out for a meal I shared a bit with him about my life and he told me that my story would make a good book so that was how it started," Andrew explained.

"Kimberly and Sarah read it. The book about your life I mean. They can't stop talking about it! Sorry, I hope you don't take offence but I simply don't read many novels," confessed George scratching his cheeks while making a sweeping gesture.

"None taken. I…" Andrew exhaled a deep breath. He bit his lip, contemplating whether he wanted to disclose which of the storylines of the book were about him. He glanced at the coffee cup while playing with the teaspoon.

George looked at him, confused as to why Andrew had stopped in the middle of his sentence. Just as George was about to open his mouth to say something, he saw Andrew readying himself to resume the story.

"You see, I… I'd a son when I was nineteen," Andrew halted and when he spoke again, his voice was quiet and sombre. "His name was Nathan…" Even after all those years, he was still uncomfortable talking about his son, especially to someone who at that point was still a stranger.

George sat there in anticipation of what Andrew was going to say next.

"He went to study in the US and was killed in a car accident," said Andrew quickly. "After I was notified, I flew over there to arrange his funeral and brought back his ashes."

"Oh! I'm very sorry to hear that and about what you went through. It must be the worst and hardest experience for any parent," said George, offering a rueful smile. Though he recognised the storyline was based on what had already been summarised by Kimberly and Sarah, it was a profound experience to hear it from Andrew. He was able to sense the pain of Andrew when he talked about his son.

"There was also one part of the book about my previous relationship…" Looking reflective, Andrew lightly tapped his fingers on the table.

"Oh."

"I'm sure Kimberly and Sarah have gathered from reading the novel that I'm gay and the novel also included a plot about my last failed relationship." As soon as the last word left his mouth, Andrew's posture relaxed. After all, he was in his early fifties and felt comfortable in his own skin. He didn't think coming out to anyone should be a big issue at this point.

"Sorry about that. I mean about the failed relationship, not about you being gay!" George almost bit his tongue hastily trying to clarify what he really wanted to say.

"No worries! I know what you meant." Andrew nodded.

"Hope you don't mind me asking. Did they sell well? I mean those two novels of his?" asked George curiously.

"Well his first novel, the one based on his own life and family sold better and as it happened it was turned into a movie. The second one, based on my life, didn't do so well, unfortunately."

"Oh, that is a shame. I'll ask Sarah and Kimberly to look out for the first one and the DVD though!" chipped in George.

"I'll get you one and also a signed copy of the novel," Andrew offered. A sudden exhaustion fell on him after talking about the novels and he desperately wanted to change the subject.

"Ta. Kind of you. I'm sure we'll enjoy watching it."

"Be prepared to be emotional and for lots of heartbreaking twists and tears!" cautioned Andrew with a smile.

"Thanks for the info. Sarah would tell you that men, she meant me, usually are not emotionally engaged with films. And she assumes that men don't talk about or show their emotions enough. Though nothing is ever enough. Don't you think?" George joked and they both laughed.

Andrew glanced at their cups and looked up at George. "Refill?"

"Sure, but first I need to use the facilities. As I get older my bladder has either shrank like a pea or enlarged. Whatever it is, I now need to pee more often, especially after drinking coffee! Usually, I drink Coke." George laughed loudly as he stood up and motioned towards the loo.

Andrew chuckled at George's bluntness.

When Andrew came back holding one cup of coffee and a large glass of Coke he saw George was already sitting in his chair.

"Here." Andrew placed the glass in front of George. He took a sip of his coffee enjoying the taste and aroma.

"Oh, my mum sends her regards. She was thrilled that we're meeting up," said George.

"Thanks. How is she and how is she coping?"

"Aye, my Mum, she's fine…" Taking a sip of the Coke, George looked down; breathing deeply in, betraying a sign of hesitation about whether it was too soon to talk about his family situation. He raised his eyes gently looking at Andrew and somehow found the courage and ease to share his past with him. He began to tell his tale. A tale that he'd managed to gather together bit by bit as an adult through talking to Aileen on multiple occasions. Once George was comfortable talking about it, there was no stopping him.

"You see; Aileen isn't my real mum. My birth mother was called Freya. Aileen is my father's second wife. My birth mother committed suicide when I was about two. Unfortunately, I don't know much about her because my old man never wanted to talk about her. Also, the chances of talking to him about it have diminished now with his condition."

Without noticing, Andrew's jaw dropped and he sat with his mouth open in shock for a long time. Listening to George Andrew could feel the deep-rooted agony. He wanted to say something to show his empathy, something to let George know he cared but he was lost for words, other than repeating the phrase 'That's horrible!'

"You see, my mother suffered from mental health issues due to what happened to her during the war. In those days there was less compassion and understanding of the issues in society and fewer treatments were available and offered, especially to women. Kimberly told me she read books about survivor's guilt and I'm pretty sure that was what ate my mother alive. Her first husband and their son were killed during the war."

"I'm truly sorry. I'm lost for words," admitted Andrew, shaking his head.

"My old man met Aileen and got married to her in 1966, about a year after my birth mother's suicide. At that time, I was in foster care. After they got married, I was finally brought home to live with them permanently. I don't remember much of that because I was only a bit older than three."

"How was Ail... Aileen, was she..." Andrew awkwardly stumbled over his words at the sensitive nature of it all.

"She has been a great mother and the only mother I know," George jumped in to answer Andrew's question knowing exactly what he wanted to ask despite his difficulty formulating it.

"I'm glad," stated Andrew.

"She was married and had a boy with her ex-husband before their divorce. But that is a story for another time," sighed George.

Suddenly a growling sound came from Andrew's stomach. "Oh, sorry, I haven't had any breakfast today!" declared Andrew while rubbing his belly.

"I'm peckish as well. Wouldn't mind having a bite to eat."

"Should we have lunch here? My treat!" offered Andrew. He glanced at George waiting for his reply.

"Good idea. Thanks. Let me text Sarah but first I need to answer nature's call. I have to use the loo again," bluntly announced George, while he hastily got up from his seat.

As the afternoon went on, they continued their talk till George eventually stifled a silent yawn. "This is the price you pay for getting older! I missed my nap today," he declared as he stretched out his arms and then yawned again.

"You keep saying you're old. The fifties are the new thirties!" Andrew protested.

"Aye, aye, for you trendy people maybe. Oh, you mentioned before that you want to visit my father in the care home. I'll arrange it and let you know, OK? Listen, my mum and Sarah would also love to meet you. I'll organise a dinner and invite you over and bring your friend or significant other along… that is if you dare to come to the poorer part of the city!" joked George, enjoying his own banter with a laugh as they parted.

About a week later, Andrew and George met outside the care home where Steve was residing.

"Hi, cuz, just to warn you my father may not remember about your father. I'm not sure he even knew you existed. He seldom recognises us but always feels at ease when we're around, especially in my mum's presence."

"I understand. I don't really expect him to know who I am," confessed Andrew.

"He's now in the advanced stages of dementia with other health complications too. You'll need to speak louder than usual to him as he has also lost his hearing a bit," explained George while entering the care home.

Andrew followed.

The receptionist recognised George and greeted him.

"My cousin," George introduced Andrew, pointing at him.

After they had been registered, George led Andrew to Steve's private room. First, they passed a lounge and a dining room before they entered a corridor where Andrew saw a few care home residents waiting under some kind of signs. As he looked closer he noticed the corridor had been redecorated with signs from banks, bus stops and mini food stores.

"This is to help them for brief moments to go back to their former lives or where they once worked," explained George who saw the questioning look on Andrew's face.

Andrew nodded.

"Look over there." George discreetly pointed to a woman sitting in an armchair embracing and gently talking to a baby doll.

They then turned right after the corridor where there were "private homes" for each resident. Outside a door Andrew saw a sign, *Steve Hughes*. Suddenly Andrew's heart was pounding in anticipation of meeting his uncle for the first time.

"Here we are!" George opened the door and entered and Andrew followed.

"Dad, how are you? Guess who I've with me today?" announced George to the elderly Steve, who was sitting straight up on his bed with a pillow at his back. A care home staff member had just finished feeding him lunch.

The staff member greeted them with a smile as she recognised George. "Your son is here to see you Steve and he brought a friend with him," said the staff member close to Steve's ear while she wiped his mouth with a napkin.

"My cousin." George tilted his head slightly in Andrew's direction.

The staff member nodded and looked at them both. "I'm done here. I'll leave you. Your father didn't eat much today." She left the room carrying a tray along with her.

As she passed, Andrew noticed there was still lots of food untouched on the plate.

George and Andrew sat in two armchairs close to the bed and George started speaking loudly to Steve about Andrew and how they found each other.

Steve seemed to be listening but was not responsive.

George turned his head and gave Andrew an apologetic look then turned his attention back to Steve.

"Mum told me to bring this for you." George took out a sweater from his bag and put it next to Steve. "Mum knitted it for you. Isn't it nice?" George held it up high and showed it to Steve and then to Andrew.

With a blank stare, Steve still didn't show any sign of being responsive.

"She'll be here tomorrow to see you." George placed the sweater next to Steve's bed.

Witnessing George's interactions with Steve, Andrew could only admire his patience and was about to make a remark when he heard George start reporting to Steve about Kimberly.

"Kimberly and her family will be coming back to Edinburgh during Christmas and she can't wait to see you," said George as he patted Steve's hand. For that brief moment, George became philosophical. He had never been close to his dad growing up because Steve never made any great effort to bond with him. It was almost unthinkable to imagine he could be talking to his father so tenderly and holding his hand.

Suddenly a strong putrid smell from Steve's bed drifted across the room, an odour of stools. Before Andrew could figure out where the smell came from that was penetrating his nose, George stood up swiftly and walked to the night table next to the bed and pressed a bell.

"Sorry. I've pressed the bell for a staff member to come to change my old man," remarked George, visibly embarrassed.

"Don't worry about it." Andrew shook his head.

Steve was totally unaware of the situation despite the odour becoming persistent and even stronger.

George waited for a few minutes but it felt as the time stood still as the lingering smell became stronger. As his embarrassment grew, George finally lost his patience and was about to press the bell again. His finger froze in the air for a few brief seconds but then he withdrew it and rushed out of the door instead. "Wait here, I'll be back."

Andrew was left alone with Steve, a scenario he had never imagined a few weeks ago before Kimberly had contacted him.

He looks exhausted, as if the life has been sucked out of him. A sudden sadness overcame Andrew. He took a closer glance at him. Steve was skeletally skinny and had a hollow look in his eyes lying in his bed undisturbed and unaware of what just happened. Andrew studied him further and noticed Steve had protruding white hair coming out of his nose and ears. Andrew spotted veins popping through his pale translucent skin.

Before coming, Andrew had been wondering in his head whether he would see any resemblance to his father when he saw Steve. Then he laughed at his own thoughts because even if the two brothers bore some similarity to each other he did not really know what his father looked like.

How foolish of me. I would not be able to recognise my own father if he were to stand in front of me now. I only saw a few photos of him when he was in his twenties and he left when I was an infant.

As Andrew leaned in close to Steve all the while the strong odour coming from him intensified. Andrew recoiled and made a gagging sound. He covered his mouth with his hand, trying his best not to throw up. His face was burning with embarrassment as he stood up and quickly walked away from Steve towards the window and opened it. He let out a breath and noticed a pot of blooming orchids and photos of his family placed on a small coffee table under the window.

"Uncle Steve. These are your family," said Andrew pointing at the photos he held in his hand.

Steve was close-lipped and did not look at where Andrew was pointing.

"Uncle Steve, it would have been so nice to have met you earlier so that you could tell me more about you and my father growing up." Andrew tried again hoping to catch Steve's attention.

"I don't want to live any longer." A faint voice came seemingly from nowhere.

Andrew jumped a bit in surprise at the sudden noise. As Andrew looked closer he figured out it was Steve who had mumbled. Staring at Steve, Andrew was uncertain how to respond.

"What?" Andrew was unsure he had heard correctly. He walked closer to Steve.

"I don't want to live any longer," Steve weakly repeated, this time just loud and clear enough for Andrew to understand. He turned his head now looking at Andrew with his hollow eyes.

Andrew still didn't respond, as he didn't know how.

"I've had enough. I don't want to live any longer," Steve repeated again, articulate with his words this time. He started to breathe and exhale unevenly.

"Don't say that! George will be back with a nurse soon to make you more comfortable." Andrew was quite close to Steve yet he realised he was almost shouting when speaking to Steve. The only thing in his mind at that moment was how to calm Steve a little.

"Who are you?"

"I'm Andrew. You're brother to my father Neil. You're my uncle."

Steve raised an eyebrow looking at Andrew with suspicion. Either he didn't believe Andrew or did not understand what Andrew had said.

They stared at each other for a few moments not knowing what to say to each other.

Andrew cleared his throat. "Let's make a deal. I'll come and celebrate your next birthday and we can talk some more. I believe you'll be eighty-seven next year!" Andrew said in a cheerful voice.

Steve seemed to be unsure but Andrew could see a glimmer of understanding in his eyes.

"Birthday, whose birthday?" asked Steve in a low tone.

"Yours. I'll come to celebrate your next birthday, if you'll invite me!" Andrew gave a cheeky smile.

Steve's facial expression softened and he grinned for a second but it disappeared before it was really visible. He turned his head away from Andrew.

"We're here!" George rushed back, short of breath. A staff member appeared after him. George approached Andrew, tapped on his shoulder and led him out of the room for the staff member to change Steve's diapers.

While waiting outside the room, Andrew shared with George the moment he thought he'd briefly connected with Steve about celebrating his next birthday.

"That is a promise. You're definitely invited. I'll tell the story to my mum!" said George with an astonished expression beaming on his face.

Andrew hailed a taxi outside and dropped George off at his home first.

Once the taxi was heading towards his place, Andrew thought about his earlier experiences with people living with dementia. His best friend Jimi's father, Mr Wang, had also suffered from it before his passing. Andrew and his mother visited him numerous times when he lived in the care home. Also, Andrew used to volunteer in a day centre for people living with this disease. He'd witnessed first-hand the pain and suffering of those living with dementia and their families.

Andrew visited Steve again in early January 2020 and that was the last time he saw him. The first lockdown restrictions had begun on 23rd March 2020 so he never got to celebrate Steve's birthday. In December 2020, Steve contracted COVID-19 and died soon after. Andrew learned from George that the whole experience was awful, especially for Aileen. She was traumatised not to be able to see or visit him before he died. At that time Scotland was in total lockdown because of fear of the spread of the virus.

Andrew couldn't attend the funeral because it was strictly reserved for close family members in order to comply with the lockdown restrictions imposed by the Government.

Chapter 6 – 2021/2022

Kimberly and her family, along with Aileen, had their Christmas and New Year holiday celebrations in George and Sarah's place where Kimberly and her family had been staying. A few days before she was to go back to Aberdeen after the holiday celebrations, she brought her kids to visit Aileen. They had to squeeze themselves past boxes in the hallway to enter the living room. Kimberly was mortified when she saw even more boxes and bags, some of them half-packed, scattered around the living room. She couldn't believe the disarray inside Aileen's home.

"What are these?" queried Kimberly looking at Aileen and then turning her attention towards her kids when she saw them running around playing hide and seek between the boxes. "Be careful! Don't knock down the boxes!"

"They were clothing items and belongings of your granddad that I'm sorting out," replied Aileen, seemingly embarrassed.

"But, why are they still here?" asked Kimberly, her disbelief evident on her face.

"As you know, your granddad died in December 2020 during the first lockdown. After that was eased somewhat, your mum and dad came to help but we had only got to the tip of the iceberg. Then the second lockdown was imposed again and we were not allowed to socialise or visit each others' homes so—"

"I thought one's nearest were able to visit each other?" interrupted Kimberly.

"To tell you the truth, I don't remember now. I was so confused with the various household and social distancing restrictions during and between each lockdown," Aileen declared and let out a sigh. "I felt like the whole pandemic never happened in a strange way, like the period of two years was just voided from my life."

"But the boxes are still here?" Kimberly posed her question again.

"Yes. I had only started sorting and packing again after the visit of Alistair and Michelle. Your dad did offer a few times to help but you know with his bad knees it's almost impossible for him to manoeuvre around those boxes and lifting or bending down is out of the question. It's unfair to put him through it."

"Don't worry, I will come down to help you. In the meantime, you have to be careful not to fall over them, Nan. You promise?" said Kimberly in her parting words.

In February of 2022, Kimberly took a few days off from work to come back to Edinburgh alone to help Aileen with sorting out and packing Steve's belongings.

Another reason that made Kimberly come back sooner than planned was that Aileen had had problems with her balance recently and consequently had fallen a few times. Luckily, she wasn't seriously hurt apart from a few bruises on her head and a twisted ankle.

After Kimberly arrived Aileen had told her that once Alistair learned about her fall he had suggested she either move into a care home or come to live with them in California, an offer he persistently repeated. Both suggestions were firmly declined by her.

"I am still managing well on my own. Alistair has decided to come back to Edinburgh in a few weeks' time to have further discussions with me and your father. But, I am not moving anywhere," firmly voiced Aileen.

Kimberly nodded but was preoccupied with all the boxes in front of her. Looking around, she was half amused and half shocked that the disorder displayed inside her grandma's home seemed to be worse than she remembered from the time she was there last with her kids. That was just before she returned home to Aberdeen after the Christmas and New Year celebrations.

"Nan, I'm surprised you could live like this! This is a hazard zone and it's really dangerous! No wonder you have fallen multiple times. Have you tried to pack more since I saw you last?" asked Kimberly in amazement, pointing at all the boxes and bags.

"Only a bit. Your mum was here last weekend to help," said Aileen, not disclosing how much pain she was still suffering from her twisted ankle, knowing it would only escalate Kimberly's worries.

"Tell me where I should start!"

"Why don't you start by going through those boxes in the hallway and then move them into the second bedroom? It will make getting in and out much easier,' suggested Aileen. Aided by a walking stick, Aileen walked carefully and sluggishly back to the living room and sat down in an armchair. "Phew!" Aileen heaved a sigh of relief.

For the next few days, Kimberly stayed over at Aileen's place and helped her sort out, pack and repack things for donation to charity shops or to be thrown out. Sarah and George came by as well a few times though most of the time it was team Kimberly and Aileen. While working they also enjoyed their grandma-granddaughter time together.

"Now we're getting somewhere!" declared Kimberly as she sat on the living room sofa next to Aileen, drinking tea, looking around and beaming with pride.

"Dear, can you bring the suitcase from my bedroom?"

"Which one?" Kimberly asked before going to Aileen's room.

"The black one next to the dresser!"

Kimberly came back with the suitcase, looking at Aileen for further instructions.

"I set some clothes aside for Cameron thinking maybe he might like them. They'll certainly not fit your father."

Kimberly opened and went through the suitcase and pulled out some jumpers and similar items, a few even unworn and still with price tags on.

"Wow, this one looks nice and good quality too! I reckon it'll fit Cameron quite well," praised Kimberly as she examined a thick woollen tweed overcoat more closely and ran her fingers over the fabric.

Putting the coat on, Kimberly stood in front of a full-length mirror in the hall outside Aileen's bedroom. As she spun around and admired it she became sentimental because she recognised a hint of her granddad's aftershave that he had frequently worn. She quickly composed herself before she walked back to the living room still with the coat on.

"If I remember correctly, I bought it for your granddad on his seventy-fifth birthday. It's good quality and keeps its shape well. When your granddad found out how much I paid for it he said I should just give him the money instead! Typical of your granddad," joked Aileen, shaking her head. "It has been inside the suitcase for a while now so Cameron might want to wash it first. I mean dry cleaning, of course."

"I'm sure Cameron will love it," said Kimberly and at the same time she put her hands inside the pockets. "Oh, there is quite a large hole inside this pocket!" She pulled the pocket inside out, showing it to Aileen.

"Erm, your granddad never mentioned it!" she replied.

"Imagine if something fell through the hole! Or better yet, some money!" bantered Kimberly. She bent down slightly and patted inside the tartan lining fabric. Her hand slowly moved around and stopped suddenly as her face froze.

"What? What's the matter?" asked Aileen as she observed Kimberly's expression of amazement.

"There *is* something inside, trapped between the tweed and the lining!" said Kimberly, overcome with curiosity.

"Really? What could it be?" asked Aileen. She leant forward in her armchair, looking genuinely surprised.

Kimberly took off the coat and laid it on the coffee table. She reinserted her hand deep into the hole and pulled out what she'd found and showed it to Aileen.

Aileen was stunned. What Kimberly had found were photos.

"Who are these people?" asked Kimberly. For some unknown reason her heart rate was racing and she felt a sudden dryness in her mouth.

Aileen went through the photos. A few of them were of a couple holding an infant. She only recognised one person in the photo, her husband, Steve.

"This young man was your granddad, the infant was your father, and this lady, she must be Freya, your father's birth mother. Today is the first time I have seen what she looked like..."

Kimberly kept quiet, waiting on Aileen for further explanation.

"Yes, these are of your father's birth mother. But your granddad told me that he destroyed and burnt all photos of Freya after her death!" exclaimed Aileen in surprise at the fact that any pictures of Freya existed.

"Unbelievable! My goodness, she's so thin," Kimberly remarked as she held the photos with care and closely studied them.

Aileen nodded.

"I have never seen photos of my father at this young age. He must've been not more than one," said Kimberly in astonishment.

"Wait, who is this?" Aileen saw another small fragile and torn photo with a faded image of an infant.

Kimberly looked at Aileen with the same puzzled expression.

Aileen turned the photo and saw faint writing in ink on the back – 'Tomer geboren 18. Juli 1939.'

Aileen showed it to Kimberly and without saying anything Kimberly checked her phone for a translation.

"It means Tomer born on 18th July 1939," Kimberly confirmed.

"Born in July 1939. Could it be…?" asked Aileen under her breath.

Suddenly Aileen raised her head and met Kimberly's eyes. They had a strong inkling about who the baby boy was but both were too stunned to say it to each other. The discovery sent a chill up their spines. But what they didn't know at that moment was that Freya had committed suicide on the 18th of July 1965, twenty-six years later on the same date as Tomer's birthday.

"Just to be sure, check about the name Tomer." Aileen pulled Kimberly's arm to get her attention.

"Check what, Nan? I'm not sure what you want me to do!"

"The Jewish name Tomer, or Tomer in Hebrew, does it have any connection with the name Thomas?" The words rushed out of her mouth in a jumble, Aileen anticipated Kimberly would understand what she was hinting at.

"Nan, what do you mean?" asked Kimberly in complete surprise because she had never seen Aileen in such an excitable state.

"Maybe it's far-fetched but check if Tomer means Thomas in Hebrew, or in the Jewish tradition or however you put it!" Aileen's eyes lit up in excitement hoping Kimberly would give her the answer she was looking for.

Kimberly did the search on her phone and quickly confirmed, "Yes, Nan, Thomas is Tomer in Hebrew which means palm tree."

Aileen let out a long sigh and was speechless for a moment.

Suddenly Kimberly understood what Aileen had been looking for. George's full name was George Thomas Hughes. Freya named George after her first son. The wee boy in the photo was George's half-brother. He was Freya's first son, who had perished during the Holocaust.

For a while, Kimberly and Aileen looked at each other and then stared at the photo without being able to find the words to describe their feelings about what they'd found.

"Wait, I think there is something more inside," announced Kimberly, turning the jacket upside down to make sure nothing was still trapped inside between the tweed and the lining.

"Don't scare me. I'm not sure my heart can bear more surprises." Aileen put her hand over her chest.

Kimberly revealed what she found to Aileen and both looked puzzled.

"What on earth would your granddad save these torn postcards for?"

"Beats me," said Kimberly, shaking her head as she turned the cards around. "Oh, it says here they were paintings of Vincent van Gogh."

"Did someone send them to him?"

"No, they're unused and new, well they're now torn. Mean anything to you, Nan?"

"No clue whatsoever. Imagine your granddad, an art appreciator?" joked Aileen and they both burst into laughter but stopped simultaneously feeling disrespectful at that moment towards what they had discovered.

"Maybe they belonged to Freya?" Kimberly looked at Aileen without being able to contribute anything further because she was too bewildered at finding the mysterious postcards in addition to the photos.

"Call your father to come over," said Aileen and sat straight in the armchair with an elated expression on her face at imagining how glad George would be that those photos were found.

Without any hesitation, Kimberly phoned her father and asked him to come right away. Her heart was pounding, full of anticipation of her father's reaction when he saw those photos. *It will mean the world to him to see what his mum and his half-brother looked like, finally.*

While Kimberly was talking to George on the phone, Aileen was flooded with a mixture of sentiments including feeling troubled about Steve's intentions with those pictures. *Did Steve hide those photos there so they could be found? Or did he forget he put them there? How are the postcards related to everything? What a lucky coincidence that Kimberly found them. Imagine if they had thrown away the jacket...*

Chapter 7 – 2022

It wasn't an understatement to say that George was both shocked and pleased at the same time when Aileen handed him the photos Kimberly found. He was amazed to see for the first time the images of his birth mother and his half-brother, whom they believed he was named after.

After his initial reaction of joy and excitement, tightly holding those photos, George couldn't help getting frustrated with his dad.

Fuck. What was my old man playing at? How could he be so careless and tell no one about the photos? Are there other photos or additional items still to be found?

The thought of his father hiding those photos wore on him, more so because he was no longer able to confront him about his reasoning. He got even angrier when he thought that those photos could have easily been lost forever if his father's coat had been given to a charity shop or at least damaged if Cameron had sent it to a dry cleaner's.

Had he ever acknowledged I was a victim too? Had he ever wondered how the past affected me? George was bewildered and troubled with these questions racing through his head for days. At times he was uneasy at being furious with his own dad because he was also sympathetic towards him considering how difficult and painful it had all been for him.

George now had bags under his eyes and was constantly exhausted and tired, with great difficulty falling asleep and waking up. Many times he woke up with his fist clenched tightly and unable to open by itself. He had to use his other hand to release it one finger at a time. It had been a painful exercise because his hand had been held in the same position for the whole night. Also, his mood was worsening caused by his battle with weight gain. This not only made him self-conscious but also caused his health and confidence to deteriorate further. George blamed it on the lockdown but he kept piling on even more after the dreadful saga was over. Increasingly, he had difficulty breathing, especially while sleeping. He was short of breath when walking for too long and he often complained about the pain in his back and knees, which persisted.

Lack of sleep and the health issues caused by his weight gain made him feel that everything was dull and he experienced sudden mood swings, noticeable even at work where he became increasingly sensitive.

George shared the news about the discovery of the photos with some colleagues he regarded as close. At first they were sympathetic towards him but soon enough he noticed they would cut their conversations short, especially when he started complaining over and over again about his father. From his point of view, people should be more considerate; in addition to adjusting to coming out of the lockdown, he was also processing his anger towards his father and the lingering issues related to his birth mother's death which he never had a chance to process. He felt that his colleagues had begun walking on eggshells and acting awkwardly around him, for some reason he failed to grasp. He felt deflated as no one cared to really listen to him about his manifold struggles.

Why do people avoid me at work? George struggled to understand, without realising that their reaction to him was merely a reflection of him being overly needy, constantly requiring others to listen and agree with him.

"Don't overthink it. They might be dealing with issues of their own," comforted Sarah, but she knew well that no one wanted to become burdened with another's troubles and be an emotional punching bag, especially since everyone was facing up to the aftermath of the pandemic. It was something Sarah understood well because after returning to work she noticed her own need for space and felt uncomfortable at being closely surrounded by colleagues and customers.

In addition to managing his disappointment with his colleagues, Sarah also became aware that George was particularly annoyed and upset with a neighbour called Bob he thought they'd got on well with.

George and Bob befriended each other during the lockdown period. They obeyed the household bubble rule and only met outside a few times a week. Chatting to Bob was something George looked forward to. During their short walks, they often vented to each other about their frustration over the COVID restrictions. As much as they both understood the importance of following rules to protect others they had the same sentiment about government ministers telling people to stay home.

"It's easy for them to tell us to stay home! These ministers most likely live in big houses with access to gardens. To keep our mental health intact we need to get out and have human interactions but we're made to feel guilty about it!" complained Bob during one of their walks while George nodded his head in total agreement.

The two of them even co-organised a drinks event for the residents living in the building between lockdowns. Most of the neighbours attended the event. Still complying with the social distancing restrictions, they scattered around the entrance hallway with their own drinks. Sarah had seldom seen George so alive. He brought his old CD player along and was ecstatic at being in charge of providing music throughout the event. The building was filled with much-needed laughter when people had a sing-along to ABBA songs. George truly enjoyed the event, partly through being able to socialise and feel somewhat 'normal' again, but also because he felt like he was needed and, most importantly, that he was appreciated.

After the success of the event, George and Bob enthusiastically discussed organising other social events in the future. They also talked about going out for dinner along with Sarah when the lockdown was lifted.

"Wonder what he's up to? He's been very quiet for a few days. He hasn't replied to my recent messages," pondered George, referring to Bob after the lockdown restrictions were finally lifted.

"Must be busy now the restrictions have eased," said Sarah, shrugging her shoulders. She didn't even look up. She was busy folding the laundry on the kitchen table and not paying too much attention to George.

One day after work while walking up to his flat, in an attempt to lose weight, George saw two flowerpots outside Bob's flat.

"These flowers look like they need watering," mentioned George to Sarah as soon as he got home.

Sarah shrugged her shoulders without replying because at that moment her mind was preoccupied with the never-ending court case against her brother. She also had no understanding of why George was troubling himself with other people's flowerpots.

"Don't interfere," Sarah warned when George seemed to want to continue talking about it.

After keeping an eye out for a few days, George sent a text message again to Bob asking what he was up to. George also mentioned the sorry-looking flowers he'd seen and that he would be happy to take care of them. A reply quickly came from Bob this time, politely informing George that he was in London attending a conference and should be back after the weekend and thanking George for thinking about watering the flowers but that he needn't occupy his time worrying about them.

Reading between the lines, George got the message; mind your own business. George didn't say much about it but Sarah could tell how much he was hurt and disappointed by it. She recognised how eager and involved George could be at times. The way he saw it, all he wanted was to show how much he cared for those he considered friends. George didn't reply to Bob's message because he felt rather embarrassed.

Coming home from work one day, George opened the entrance door and bumped into Bob, who was about to go out. They both greeted each other cordially and suddenly the topic popped into George's mind about the government being accused of wasting seven billion pounds buying expired and uncertified personal protective equipment during the lockdown. From their many previous discussions, George knew Bob would be happy to have a good rant about it. George enthusiastically approached Bob with a smile and was about to start the conversation when Bob put up a hand in the air as a sign to cut George off.

"Nice to see you. You look well. I'm in a rush and already late for a dinner. Let's catch up another time," said Bob while hurrying out of the building. George stood frozen in surprise for a few moments, feeling flustered at what just happened.

When George got home he shared his dismay about the incident with Sarah.

"Don't take it personally. Maybe he was just busy and had a lot of catching up to do with his friends and family," consoled Sarah when she saw how let down and disappointed George was.

No doubt George took it personally.

George grumbled more than once to Sarah that during the lockdown, though restricted by various rules and social distancing regulations, he had been fascinated to discover that people were surprisingly friendlier and had more patience. Once the lockdown was finally over and all the regulations and restrictions were lifted, when everyone got back to normal, George had difficulties adjusting. Maybe it was in his imagination but everyone seemed to be so busy again and had no time to greet each other or chat.

George called Aileen and told her what had happened with Bob. To cheer him up, she invited him over for lunch one day where George took the opportunity to pour out his discontentment to Aileen.

"People took time, stopped in the street and greeted each other. We looked out for each other's parcels and helped with the recycling bins in our building. Doesn't it count for anything? I mean I got to know more of our neighbours during that period than ever before. Don't you agree?"

"Love, don't put too much stock in it. Give them space. Normally people don't greet each other on the street unless you know them," observed Aileen. "People are just getting on with their lives plus they also have their own friends and family they need to see. Also, they're adjusting back to their old ways of doing things from before the pandemic."

"I know. Everyone is busy," mumbled George.

Just as George was about to move on from his disappointment with Bob he found himself in a tricky position on the work front. He only briefly mentioned it to Sarah because she was already troubled with the court case with her brother about their father's estate after his passing and George didn't want to burden her with his work problem. He called Kimberly for her perspective hoping she would have a better understanding of the delicate position he was in.

"Hey, how are you? Oh, I have good news for you. I finally managed to get my act together and found a photo shop that could repair the photos we found," Kimberly happily reported.

"Oh, great. Hmm…"

"What's wrong?" asked Kimberly, knowing her father well enough to sense he was troubled by something.

"Erm. I… I'm in a pickle of a situation at work," he revealed, sounding deflated.

"What happened? It can't be that bad."

George started telling Kimberly about his dilemma.

In the beginning of 2020, around two months before the first COVID wave had arrived in UK, George had been invited to take part in an interview panel for new applicants at his department. It was a boost for George's confidence because he felt that he was finally appreciated. He wasted no time contemplating questions in his head and even what he should wear to the interview.

"I told you about the interview before. I'm submitting suggestions for questions to my line managers," explained George when Sarah saw him concentrating hard on making notes in the kitchen one evening after their tea.

Looking at George, Sarah's eyes twinkled. She knew how much it meant for George to be asked because he was often overlooked for any promotions at work. George was never good at office politics nor was he good with people skills. He was too black and white and nothing in between. He often spoke his mind, which was not always well-received at work or in his private life. Many times he had put himself in a difficult position because, without him noticing it, some people perceived his bluntness and his natural eagerness to please as well as his quirky sense of humour as a weakness and took advantage of it.

George was beaming when the interview process went well, especially after the young candidate he recommended was hired. The new colleague, Bryan, joined the team where George worked and looked up to George. George enjoyed it and prided himself on being a mentor and showing him the ropes.

Not long after Bryan joined, the first lockdown happened and George and Bryan kept in reasonably good contact during the period of restrictions. George called a few times to check on Bryan, making sure he was receiving the furlough scheme payments like any other employee during that difficult time. George also met up with Bryan in person twice, though strictly speaking they were not supposed to due to regulations at that time against mixing with different households, even if meeting outside. They met at St Andrew's Square and walked several circuits in the cold drizzling rain while George patiently lent an ear to Bryan who shared his difficulties on the home front, living in a one-bedroom flat with his girlfriend and their baby.

As they were classified as front-line workers, they were asked to go back to work in their workplace at an early stage. No one knew why but Bryan was asked to transfer to another department for a while when they first went back to work. George and Bryan kept in contact through occasional calls and text messages and after some time Bryan informed George that he was to come back to his original team. To welcome him back, George invited Bryan and his girlfriend over for a meal when the socialising restrictions had eased somewhat. During the dinner, George and Bryan cheerfully talked about how great it was to work in the same team again.

Shortly after Bryan had been reunited with the team George saw a change in him and, worse yet so did other colleagues. Before long it was on everyone's lips and they began making comments about Bryan behind his back, about him being often late to work and spending quite a lot of time on his phone and not being as committed to the work as he used to be. They hinted that George should talk to him because word got around that it was George who had originally recommended him for the job after his interview.

"That is so unfair of them to pressure you!" stated Kimberley as George recounted his tale. "They should not ask you to bear the burden of talking to him. Did you talk to Mum about it?"

"Aye. I did, but very briefly," he responded.

"What did she say?"

"Like you, that I should not be pressured into talking to Bryan. I should report it to my manager."

"I can't agree more. You should keep your nose out of it. Don't get involved because you don't know for sure what is going on in Bryan's life. You are walking in dangerous territory. In the end, it's not your battle to fight. It sounded like your colleagues wanted to put you on the front line of gaslighting the situation. Don't fall for it," warned Kimberly, at that moment sounding like her mother. She shook her head in disgust, appalled by the behaviour of George's colleagues.

George coughed drily to disguise being ill at ease.

"Don't do anything hasty before you talk to me or Mum. Dad, I mean it," firmly conveyed Kimberly firmly, worried and wanting to make sure George understood her concern.

After the call with Kimberly, George reflected on Sarah often teasing him about not being able to hide his likes and dislikes well and people being able to read his emotions like an open book. He had always been passionate about helping people but not everyone saw his good intentions and it could come back to bite him.

The next day, George went back to work still indecisive about Bryan. He basically agreed with Sarah and Kimberly not to get involved and not to interfere. However, the gossip about Bryan among his colleagues intensified in the next few days. In the end, George just couldn't bear the thought of others making such mocking comments about the poor man without him knowing.

With the best intentions in his mind, George approached Bryan. Much to his relief, Bryan was not upset and even thanked George for taking the time to talk to him. He also said that he was dealing with private matters at home and adjusting to coming back to work. George was pleased that the conversation went well and promised to provide support when needed. After the talk for a few days, Bryan showed up at work on time and the quality of his work improved but it was short-lived and all the talk and mocking comments about Bryan's lack of work ethic quickly resurfaced.

One person who was greatly affected and disturbed by the development was George. Not thinking twice about it, George took the initiative to talk to Bryan again. George invited Bryan to lunch, where George brought up what was on his mind and also revealed what the other colleagues were saying about him behind his back about his performance at work.

With his forehead furrowed Bryan was quiet throughout the conversation. He only took a few bites of his favourite dish, bangers and mash. He kept his head down, biting his lips and his whole facial expression was frozen in a frown. George interpreted it that Bryan was mulling over things and was receptive to what he had shared with him. George was mightily pleased with himself and glad that Bryan seemed to be taking his well-intended advice on board.

Two days after that conversation, George was called into the HR office. A first-stage complaint of harassment had been made by Bryan against a handful of colleagues, with an emphasis on a case against him. The HR team interviewed all the colleagues named in the complaint for their version of the events and told them to wait for further instructions.

Needless to say George was appalled. He robotically went back to his workstation after talking to HR but felt unwell and left work early, very unusual for George. Later that afternoon, on coming home from work Sarah found George sitting on a bench just outside their flat building looking totally shattered. It was after this incident that George's mental health deteriorated further.

"What is happening to you? Why are you sitting here and not going inside?" Sarah placed her shopping on the bench and sat next to George. With a glance, she thought George looked ten years older than that morning.

"There is a complaint about me at work," he replied morosely.

"What about? By whom?" asked Sarah in astonishment and was devastated to learn what had happened when George finally found the words to explain the ordeal at work.

I told you so. Those words rang in Sarah's head but she knew it would only aggravate the situation. What she did was comfort and convince George that HR would find nothing wrong with what he did or said. She was secretly not so sure herself though, knowing that harassment complaints could be tricky and at times not fair. She was also disheartened with Bryan. He should have known George by then. All her husband wanted was to protect him from all the gossip from the other colleagues.

George called in sick for two days and then, much to his credit, he went back to work but when the rumours about a formal in-depth investigation came out George didn't cope well and started to withdraw and not talk to anyone unless absolutely necessary or else he would unpredictably lash out for no particular reason. He was unaware of his deteriorating mental state even though the symptoms of burnout were plain to see. He experienced a feeling of hopelessness and felt as if he was detached from the world. Apart from dealing with his own personal issues about the past, including the death of his father not so long ago, there had been the negative effects of lockdown, and then the ordeal with the complaint, in addition to suffering from insomnia. It had all affected his life and his mental well-being.

Sarah witnessed close up his suffering daily and had no doubts that he needed attention from medical professionals. She made an appointment for George to see a GP and would not take no for an answer. To be sure he followed through with the visit she took a morning off to accompany George to their local medical centre. Sure enough, after seeing the GP George was asked to take a long three-week period of sick leave, for the first time in his life.

At home, during his sick leave, he had a lot of time on his hands to imagine all kinds of things. His head was preoccupied with the investigation and dwelled on the worst possible outcomes, completely out of proportion.

One evening while having their tea, George was only able to take a couple of bites before pushing the plate away. "Will they put me in jail? I mean—" he began but was interrupted.

"What are you on about again? No one is going to put you in jail! I…" Sarah hissed and was short with her husband and was too mad to finish her sentence. Her hand was shaking while holding the pepper mill as her patience stretched beyond breaking point. She put it down then stroked her hair with her fingers which reminded her that she was already in a foul mood about an unsatisfactory perm she'd just had. *Did he ever ask how my day was?* While chewing her food in silence, for a few moments Sarah was briefly distracted by the melodic sound of water dripping from the kitchen tap, which gave her the time to calm down. She moved over to the sink and tightened the tap. She asked herself how much longer she could listen to those repeated self-pitying questions from George that had already driven them both to the edge and made them rather jumpy.

George glanced at Sarah and was surprised that she'd suddenly become quiet so he picked up from where he'd been cut off. "My workplace, will they fire me? Or will I lose my pension?" George came out with his worries as he interrogated himself with a growing sense of panic and dread.

"George, you've got to stop worrying about these unrealistic outcomes!" Sarah sighed, shaking her head.

"What will people say about me when I'm not at work? How come no one cares?" George complained and sheepishly met Sarah's gaze.

Seeing George in this state broke Sarah's heart. Sarah couldn't help feeling sorry for him. She knew how much his work and colleagues meant to him. George was disheartened that after receiving a get-well card and flowers from his colleagues in his team, no one had called and asked how he was doing.

"Maybe they're best to stay out of it while the case is being investigated," Sarah offered a reasonable explanation with a rueful expression. She too was disappointed but in order not to burden her husband further she kept her sentiments to herself and only shared them with her daughter later on.

During that time one positive development was that George's state of mind improved after he started taking antidepressant drugs prescribed by his GP. Sarah felt as though she was able to breathe again, though the investigation at George's work was still hanging like a black cloud over them.

A week passed and George received a notification that the day he returned back to work from his sick leave he needed to be interviewed by an external investigator whom the company had hired to handle this case on the recommendation of the HR director. George wasn't able to sleep for a few days before the interview because he was worrying about the potential questions and how best he should provide his answers.

"They will paint me as a bad guy. Years of the hard work I've done for my job will be wiped away!" George apprehensively expressed his concern. He was also anxious about returning back to work.

"Don't anticipate all the negatives. Just tell your side of the story and see what the expert recommends," Sarah comforted.

George duly went back to work and the interview with the external investigator went smoother than he had expected. At least, despite being very nervous in the end he felt that the expert seemed to genuinely listen to his side of the story.

At work, George kept his dealings with Bryan to the minimum, avoiding him unless it was absolutely necessary. Unsurprisingly, the sentiment was mutual.

After a few weeks of fact-finding and all the parties being interviewed, the case was concluded and no misconduct was found on George's part, rather it was termed a misunderstanding. The investigator did, however, provide a recommendation that in the future all matters concerning work disputes among colleagues should be reported directly through the proper channel, namely the line manager.

Both George and Sarah were over the moon about the finding but then George fretted about how to interact with Bryan in the future. He started to fall back into a feeling of anxiety only to learn that Bryan had been transferred to another department at his own request. In a way Bryan's transfer was the best solution for everyone. However, George felt as if justice wasn't served. He doubted if any of his colleagues had stepped forward to defend him and tell the truth about how he was the one who had been pressured and harassed. But what else did he expect, for someone to be fired? He knew that wasn't what he wanted either; he was just hurt because he didn't receive the support from the HR department or his other colleagues that he thought he deserved.

"Life goes on. Everyone has their own problems to deal with. You just have to be more careful what you say and reveal at work. Your colleagues are not necessarily your friends," Sarah pointed out.

Sarah also made George aware not to set his expectations too high for others when she saw him struggling even though the case was over. She convinced him to be more cautious after the whole incident to prevent his own words from being used against him in the future. Despite his nonchalant appearance, Sarah knew George's sensitive side. One of the things she loved about her husband was his passion for helping others and his honesty because stretching the truth to get ahead at work or get along with people was never something he did. He did not like to pretend nor did he appreciate pretentious behaviour, all of which had got him in trouble in the past both at work and in his private life.

"Dad, how are you? Both Mum and I are worried about you. Mum told me you still don't sleep well and are experiencing nightmares?" Kimberly called one day to check on her dad after he started seeing a psychologist recommended by his GP, in addition to taking antidepressants.

144

"Nothing to fuss about. I just need time to process everything," claimed George and experienced a sudden itchy throat. He put down his phone and then started coughing till he was out of breath.

"Are you all right, Dad? Are you still there?" Kimberly worriedly asked. Although she pulled the phone away from her ear she was still able to hear the noise of him clearing his throat. Normally, she would have made a comment or a joke about the rather irritating sound as though he had a frog in his throat, but today she knew it wasn't the time to comment. She patiently waited.

After a while, George managed to pick up the phone and said, "Sorry about that. I'm here again. How are the kids?"

Kimberly sensed that George wasn't in the mood to talk about himself so she followed his lead and changed the subject to keep the conversation going. "Kids are fine. Cameron took them to the park."

"Grand."

"So I thought of something and would like you to hear me out," said Kimberley cautiously.

What Kimberly had in mind was for George to find out more about his birth mother and to research whether or not she had more relatives in Germany. She suggested that George should contact a TV program helping people to find and reconnect with lost family members.

"NO! Absolutely out of the question! I can't imagine anything worse than to be on TV for everyone to learn about the tragedy of our family," said George firmly, shaking his head. *What a foolish idea.*

Though George initially dismissed the idea, her reasoning and encouraging words lingered in his head, especially during his sleepless nights when he also thought about Freya and the possibility of finding other relations in Germany. *What if…*

There was no doubt that George would like more than anything in the world to find out more about his birth mother and perhaps also her other surviving relatives. Even though Aileen was an excellent loving mother to him, he'd suffered mental and emotional turmoil throughout his life. Knowing one's mother had committed suicide and growing up in a family with a father who was emotionally unavailable would be tough and painful for anyone.

After the call with her father, Kimberly had follow-up discussions with Sarah and Aileen about convincing George to find out more about Freya's life and the tragic circumstances of her death. Both of them were in agreement with Kimberly because they knew how much it would mean for George, especially since it would help him obtain a much-needed closure and maybe even new opportunities.

Aileen was pragmatically optimistic and said that she would do anything to facilitate the process from what she had gathered from Steve. However, she also didn't want to pressure George to engage in something that could further harm his already fragile mental state. She was mindful about what had happened to George at work.

Sarah had discerned that it was an area George was extremely sensitive about. He never volunteered to talk or share his feelings about it all, but being married to him for so long she knew what a great deal it would be for him to know about the past and where he came from. Nevertheless, Sarah totally grasped Aileen's concern because she was not convinced that George's mental health would cope with any findings, especially if they were unsatisfactory. Sarah also had other concerns. Even though she was a fan of the program in question and shed a tear when watching it, she did find it somewhat forced at times when the presenters often seemed too eager to make the stories more emotional and tear-filled for a happy ending.

"Kim, it's better for your father to figure out if and when he's ready. We can't force him," stated Sarah when Kimberly called to ask about George.

For a few weeks George battled in his head and the decision of whether to go ahead with Kimberly's suggestion was the only thing on his mind and even in his dreams.

"I need to know more, now that those photos have been found!" he declared one day when he came home from work. With determination in each step, he approached Sarah in the kitchen. Finally, he came to the conclusion that finding out more about Freya could provide him with a much-needed closure or perhaps even a new beginning, rather.

"Are you really sure?" Sarah looked up from setting the table in readiness for their evening tea.

"Aye. Imagine, I've other relatives in Germany from my mother's side," expressed George as he sat down. His eyes were both twinkling in wonder and sparkling with hope.

"Yes, that would be wonderful. But… are you truly ready to explore more about your life in public?" Sarah put forward her deepest concern.

"I guess so. I don't know. Well, we can apply first then we'll still have time to decide," he responded.

"That is true. Though, there is another issue that…"

"What issue?" George puzzled, looked at Sarah.

"What… what if they can't find anything or the finding is not what you're expecting? I just don't want to see you get disappointed." Sarah said as she put a hand atop George's and carefully worded her worry.

"Oh, I didn't think that far. Anyway, we can apply first and then go from there. Don't you think?" he said with hesitation in his tone, waiting for reassurance from Sarah.

"Right, I'll inform Kimberly. From what she told me, in the first stage we only need to make an online application submission. Who knows, maybe we won't be selected. And, even if we're, we could pull out at any time."

Sarah called Kimberly after they'd had their meal to inform her about George's decision. The two sat in front of the computer looking at the online submission requirements from both ends, though in fact, Kimberly was the one who took the lead with the application.

"My goodness, in addition to providing personal details, dates and locations of important family events, they're also asking us to provide documents such as photos, birth, death and marriage certificates…" Sarah pointed out.

"I know, but I think these are needed in order for the production team to make their decision and to facilitate the search if they go ahead," explained Kimberley.

While Sarah and Kimberly were busy going through the online submission process and discussing all the necessary requirements, George sat alone in the living room contemplating his decision and what it might involve.

"What are you doing in the living room?" Sarah entered, waving a list in her hand. "I've written down questions and documents we'll need from Aileen. I'll phone her tomorrow for her input."

"Oh, great," he replied.

"What's the matter?" she asked as she sensed uncertainty in his tone.

"I was thinking about Andrew. Don't you think he would be interested in participating in the same program, searching for his father who left for New Zealand when he was a toddler?" asked George and impatiently waited for Sarah to agree with what he proposed.

The idea of contacting Andrew had been circulating in his head for a few days. Besides, he would benefit from having an outsider's point of view. Andrew popped into George's mind because he believed he would understand his struggle and at the same time would be able to relate to his doubts and anticipation about researching lost family members.

"Yes... but..." she said slowly, trying to find the right words.

"But what?"

Seeing George so excited Sarah didn't have the heart to disagree with him. *Who knows, perhaps it was now as good an opportunity as ever for the two cousins to be engaged in a common project which could bring them closer.*

"Think carefully. If it goes wrong this time again you won't be able to repair the relationship with Andrew. I'm getting ready for bed now. You're coming?"

"It's only nine-thirty. I'll stay up a bit," said George and waved at Sarah who was heading to the bathroom.

George was alone again and he had a sudden urge to act and pulled out his phone to call Andrew. But just before he pressed the call button he pressed cancel instead. He was baffled how it was even harder this time to call Andrew than the first time, when he'd originally found out about him. George reflected back on Andrew and their previous meetings.

*

When George first learned about Andrew, he was over-the-moon excited to meet up and get to know him. After all, Andrew was the first relative he'd found from his father's side. Then the lockdown happened and, due to household bubble restrictions, they didn't see much of each other. Once the restrictions had eased Andrew came to their place for a meal where he met Sarah and Aileen for the first time. Both Sarah and Aileen immediately took a shine to Andrew, which pleased George. Sadly, the relationship took a different turn when George and Sarah were invited back to Andrew's place for dinner.

George was extremely excited about going to Andrew's place. He made a good effort at shaving and even wore a new sweater Sarah had bought for the occasion. After all, they were coming to the nice part of Edinburgh as he joked to Sarah.

The dinner was composed of five dishes with paired wines. Sarah enjoyed the rare fine dining experience and being pampered by Andrew. George, on the other hand, enjoyed it much less as the evening went on. At first, he was impressed and admired Andrew's penthouse flat where you could see stars from the skylight windows. He was engaged in their conversations but then his patience diminished when the first main course was served.

"Rainbow carrots! What the fuck! I never knew carrots could be anything but orange!" George quietly whined to Sarah. He pulled a face and continued with his sneering in low voice. "Really! Even the steak is cut into equal-sized cubes and I would rather have a glass of Coke!" Carelessly lifting a crystal wine glass, he almost knocked it over as he leant closer to complain to his wife. Andrew had gone to the kitchen to fetch another bottle of wine after he'd presented the dish.

"Hush now! Keep your opinion to yourself. Just enjoy and behave!" whispered Sarah with a firm tone with a quick kick under the table at George and a stare as she saw Andrew was about to come back to the table.

"Hope the steaks are to your liking?" asked Andrew, a trace of pride in his voice, while topping up their wine glasses,

Shaking his head, George forked the food around his plate making a squeaky sound. He gazed at what were supposedly edible miniscule flowers, ignoring Sarah's warning glare, and thought he must say something witty. It could be that it was the wine he drank that went to his head but George just wasn't able to restrain himself from making comments. He started by stating his appreciation to Andrew for all the trouble he had gone through in preparing the dinner but then jested that he and Sarah were simple people and such a dinner was wasted on them. Though he said it with a smile, his words implied it was all rather pretentious and showing off, or that was how Andrew perceived it at least. Ignoring Sarah kicking his leg again under the table, George then continued digging at Andrew about his delicate food served in fine-bone China, the silver cutlery and the fancy gadgets.

Keeping his feelings buried inside, Andrew felt annoyed and judged by George. Andrew had spent time studying the recipes for days and made great efforts to find suitable wine for each dish, so from his point of view he'd prepared the dinner with his best intention at heart to show how much he appreciated them. Another thing that appalled Andrew was that George had the audacity to make snide comments about his home being so neat and about his posh lifestyle. Andrew didn't appreciate the way George made him feel judged and that he constantly needed to defend himself every time they met up.

"Andrew, you've to excuse your cousin. You can't take him out anywhere!" Sarah criticised George, shaking her head with an elbow nudge to George as another warning.

They all laughed trying to defuse the awkwardness but the tension remained for the rest of the evening.

After that dinner, Sarah invited Andrew to celebrate one of the holidays with them but Andrew was travelling abroad at that time. Another dinner invitation came a few months later which Andrew also politely declined as it clashed with work commitments. Since then their contact had faded.

*

George went to the kitchen and made himself a cup of tea. He sat down and took a sip. He suddenly thought of one of Aileen's sayings 'tea makes everything better' which brought a smile to his face.

George could tell that Andrew had distanced himself after the dinner at his house. As Andrew had declined all subsequent invitations from Sarah, at that point it seemed that George was the one who had to make the effort if he were to keep any contact with Andrew, though whether or not Andrew would accept it was another story. In truth, George didn't think the evening at Andrew's went as terribly as Sarah made out. He'd grown up as an only child and he secretly longed to have a brother whom he could banter with so he wondered whether it was Andrew who was overly sensitive. What he failed to comprehend or hadn't been conscious of was that his comments and behaviour towards Andrew could be a reflection of his envy of him.

As he dwelled on it, an idea crossed his mind. He called Kimberly and asked her to message Andrew enquiring whether he would accept George's call. He waited impatiently in silence and jumped as the phone rang a little while later.

"Green light from Andrew. Can't believe he agreed to you calling this late. Good luck! Don't screw it up again," said Kimberly sternly, making sure he understood the importance of this call.

George took a long breath and exhaled slowly via his mouth and his shoulders dropped. He was hopeful that what he had to say might well be of interest to Andrew. He mulled over how his conversation with Andrew might go while he wiped off the condensation from his glasses that his hot tea had left. He dialled Andrew's number despite it being a quarter past ten.

Chapter 8 – 2022

Lying in bed, Sarah wasn't able to concentrate on reading. She had been staring at the same page for a long time, her book held absently in front of her. Her mind was focused on what George had just proposed, to contact Andrew to ask him if he would be interested in applying to search for his father alongside George's own quest.

Sarah had her reasons for her hesitation because things hadn't gone as she had hoped between George and Andrew previously. At the start, George had been very happy to have found Andrew, his first relative from his father's side. Unfortunately, the relationship turned stale after the few initial meetings through George's own doing. Though George insisted he'd had no bad intentions, not everyone understood or could take his jokes, especially when they came across as digs and personal attacks. Sarah liked Andrew and had encouraged George to call him a few times to apologise after their last dinner at Andrew's place, but George was too ashamed to admit his own misbehaviour and awkwardness.

Married to George for so many years, she had seen firsthand how George always wanted to be right, always strived to be the first, to take control and to be seen as important. He often got too involved, strived too hard to be heard, hid his vulnerability by making jokes, and was sometimes too eager to be liked and ended up being argumentative. In many ways, it reflected his hidden need to seek the approval of others. It was a way to bury his insecurities and prove to himself that he was worthy of love and respect.

Not that he wanted to admit it, but through the years Sarah had witnessed George slump into depression a few times during their marriage. That said, it was only during the recent incident at work that, at her insistence, he had seen a GP who put him on antidepressants.

Sarah had always been a supportive wife but had she ever thought about leaving him? Yes, she had, numerous times. But, she also knew her husband's positive side. His good intentions and big heart; always ready to give a hand to those in need. He volunteered in various charitable organisations and was a member of a neighbourhood watch scheme in their area. He was loyal towards his family and friends, and for those who he trusted and who showed their kindness, he would pay it back, tenfold. He had a rocky relationship with his father but he cared for and adored Aileen. He was a devoted father and grandfather and would do anything for their daughter and grandchildren. Sarah was also forever thankful to George for being so good to her parents when they were alive. Each time they needed something George was always there, the first to help, without any hesitation.

Her thoughts then wandered and she reflected on their marriage and how it took a hit during the gruelling lockdown when they were both housebound together 24/7 for a protracted period of time. Occasionally, Sarah had thought it would require a miracle for their marriage to survive. At first, she and George thought it would provide a good opportunity for them to reconnect and it so proved to be working for about ten days. Then they argued constantly over inconsequential matters and were at each other's throats. There were countless irritating events that crossed Sarah's mind when she mulled over how they and their close families had lived through the pandemic. *It was a wonder that George and I didn't kill each other.* Shaking her head, she had a giggle as she thought about some of the most ridiculous incidents.

*

One morning when Sarah had finished her breakfast and was ready for a work Zoom meeting, George stormed into the kitchen glaring around and accusing her of neglecting him, shouting about why she hadn't prepared anything for him to eat.

Another evening while they were watching TV after their tea, her ear suddenly picked up the crunching sound of George crushing ice cubes after he'd finished his drink. He had always done that but it was not until then she found this habit irritating as the sound intensified. She was about to give him a piece of her mind but then her heart softened when at the last minute she closed her eyes and decided to distract her mind by thinking about something else. As she started to feel calmer she figured out that George wasn't doing anything wrong. After all, they were living under a microscope so to speak, constantly in the eye of each other, something which had tested their patience to the limit.

There was also another remarkable incident that came to her mind. Sarah didn't recall when she started noticing that George, who was usually very careful with money, got hooked on buying scratch cards. In the beginning, Sarah thought they were simple fun, she was just annoyed with George that he didn't clean up the crumbled silvery dust after he'd scratched them. Later she also found the cards lying on the kitchen table and in the living room. Still, she didn't pay much attention till she kept seeing more and more unsuccessful scratch cards appearing in the recycling bin. Once George was in the kitchen scratching a few cards, not noticing Sarah was watching him from the hallway. She saw the intensity of his concentration as in those short moments he was distracted from all his troubles and burdens. Sarah recognised that she needed to confront him but contemplated it for a few days not knowing how to bring it up with George. The last thing she wanted was for him to feel attacked. She knew how defensive and easily offended he could be.

One evening while watching TV after their evening tea, there was a program where the presenter invited a panel consisting of a psychologist and a few guests to discuss the negative effects of the lockdowns on people.

In addition to people's mental health, the panel also mentioned that, as people stayed home more, there was a significant increase in alcohol and drug use, online gambling, impulsive online shopping due to boredom, and domestic violence. The topics of the program were of special interest to Sarah as she'd started an evening counselling course in college before the first lockdown and had continued online once restrictions were imposed. Sarah gazed at George, who seemed to be following the discussion with great attention. She knew the right moment had arrived. After the program ended she reached out and grabbed the TV remote and turned it off.

George raised an eyebrow. He turned his head and peered up at Sarah in surprise. "What—"

"George, we need to talk," interrupted Sarah, who couldn't hide the sadness in her tone.

"What? Something's the matter?"

"I think you've a gambling problem playing scratch cards," confronted Sarah, trying her best not to sound judgemental. She thought if they were to talk about it the best way was to come straight out with it rather than beating around the bush.

"What on earth are you talking about?" asked George. The comment caught him off guard and he appeared to be appalled and insulted by her accusation.

"Here!" Sarah spread all those unsuccessful cards she had collected from the recycling bin on the kitchen table. She knew George well and without any evidence, he would not admit to the problem.

The corners of George's mouth turned up but he found himself speechless. He dropped his eyes to avoid the intense stare of Sarah, visibly embarrassed. He couldn't ignore the evidence in front of him. He also couldn't help feeling belittled because Sarah had observed him without his knowledge.

Sarah was silent as well because she wanted to let everything sink in for a while. The only sound was the wall clock in the kitchen ticking.

George stood up, got himself a cup of water from the tap then walked nearer to the window. He looked outside, seemingly focused on something in the distance although it was pitch dark.

"Well, say something!" exclaimed Sarah, a hint of frustration creeping into her tone, totally forgetting all the techniques she'd learned from her counselling course. She couldn't stand the silence or George acting nonchalant like he didn't care, which increased her annoyance.

"Stop pressuring me! I will stop buying them," said George, but his voice was less than convincing.

"What is happening? Why are you wasting so much money on them?" Sarah interrogated him, barely recognising the sound of her own voice.

"I didn't waste too much," argued George, still in denial.

"Just those, I roughly counted them. Already more than 350 pounds!" Sarah got hold of the cards and threw them on the table. With her eyeballs wide open, she was taken aback at her own brusque manner but she knew it was too late to back down.

"I... I—"

"How much money have you spent buying scratch cards since the lockdown? Or had you wasted money on them even before?" Sarah asked, again cutting him off, not hiding her disappointment.

George glanced at those cards, opened his mouth to respond, but no words came out.

"Do you know that money could be put to good use for our grandchildren? Or to go towards your dental work?"

At that moment George was totally defeated. He had many fillings in his teeth and due to his strong bite, he needed frequent dental visits to repair more chips on his fillings than he or his dentist would have liked. His dentist had also strongly recommended tooth implants as well as having at least one tooth fitted with a crown but George would never give thought to it because of the high cost. Another major factor that contributing to his humiliation was that he was confronted with the fact that the money he'd wasted could've been put in the savings account of their grandchildren for the future.

Later that evening when they had calmed down, George finally revealed to Sarah that he started buying scratch cards during the second lockdown.

"Firstly for fun, a tenner here and a tenner there. But then I found that those moments of scratching the cards and finding out about the possible winnings were unexpectedly therapeutic and an escape from the daily struggles," admitted George with his head down.

From what George said, Sarah understood that those short moments of total concentration gave him a brief rush of adrenaline and he was able to forget about all his troubles and the world around him. He disclosed that he must have spent over a thousand pounds on the cards.

Being sceptical, Sarah was worried that they might have a battle to overcome for George to quit this bad habit but it took her totally by surprise that after the conversation George completely stopped buying them. In a strange way, George was relieved that he'd got caught. He heard once a saying that a problem shared is a problem halved. After he confessed his gambling problem to Sarah he felt that he didn't need to hide it or deal with it alone any longer. He still had the temptation when he saw scratch cards in shops but as soon as he remembered what Sarah said about his grandchildren he knew his money had a better purpose. George was perhaps overly proud of how he dealt with his gambling addiction and was able to move on. On the other hand, he wished his other issues could be solved as easily as he still had to deal with plenty of complications associated with all the lockdowns.

At first, during the pandemic families were not allowed to visit each other in person due to the "same household" rule but they kept close phone contact with Kimberly, Aileen and Sarah's father at that time. They all supported each other the best they could during this strenuous time. Thankfully, when the restrictions eased they were able to travel within Scotland. George and Sarah had frequent visits to Aileen and Sarah's father before he died. Sarah went and stayed with Kimberly's family a few times in Aberdeen too.

"How is Dad doing?" Kimberly had asked Sarah. "I can't believe he cancelled the trip at the last moment!" Kimberly gave her mum a hug when picking her up from the train station in Aberdeen during one of her visits.

"I can't force him. He doesn't feel comfortable taking the train surrounded by so many people, even though social distancing is in place in the train station and inside the train with everyone wearing facial coverings. Also, he feels that he needs to stay to help Aileen with sorting out all the paperwork after your granddad passed away."

"I spoke to Grandma last night. She seemed to be coping relatively well," observed Kimberly, leading Sarah to the car park.

"I can't wait to see the kids! How is Cameron doing?"

"He came back from the shop yesterday totally amazed that no one pointed out to him that he'd completely forgotten to pull up the mask from under his chin. He only thought people were looking at him strangely for whatever reason!"

"It happened to your dad a few times as well. Men!" Sarah remarked.

Both chuckled.

On their car ride back to Kimberly's, Sarah shared that she'd read a study saying that many relationships had strengthened during COVID and lockdown while many others had not survived. Married couples got divorced; couples moved away, family members, friends and colleagues fell out for one reason or another.

"I know. A friend of mine just got married before lockdown. She and her husband were quite happy at first and thought the lockdown was an opportunity to spend more quality time together. After three weeks she called me, do you know what she said?"

"I don't have the foggiest idea," said Sarah, looking intrigued.

"She said that she couldn't face having one more deep discussion! She was tired of constantly having to say something otherwise her husband would feel she was upset. Also, at one point even her husband's breathing started to sound irritating to her as well!"

"Crude, but understandable. Did I tell you I started noticing how much noise your dad makes? At one point I was annoyed about each and every sound coming from him," disclosed Sarah with a teasing tone in her voice. "A few times I had to close my eyes and count to ten to not go mad or have a rant at him!"

They laughed again.

It was during trips like this that Sarah understood that she desperately needed time away, hoping to feel some sort of normality, to feel alive. Also, they allowed her to escape from her life cramped in a small flat with George.

Once Sarah returned home from her visit to Aberdeen, the lockdown resumed. Each day became the same as the next. At times Sarah felt it was only Monday and without noticing it suddenly it was Friday. Like many people, sometimes she was bored to death but one thing she became more aware of was discussions about mental health. The topic of mental health was close to her heart because of the counselling course she'd attended and also because of the difficulties George was facing. She would discuss it with George as soon as something related to the topic was on TV, or sometimes she asked George to watch a program with her when it was on.

One evening, Sarah and George were watching a talk show on TV in which the host said that we were in the beginning of dealing with the aftermath of the lockdown, where many were starting to discover what had affected them mentally during the crisis. Some would try to avoid repeating patterns they'd picked up or developed during the lockdown. One guest in the show shared a story about her friend who said that during the first lockdown, she learned to play the piano and paint because these activities helped her deal with isolation not being able to go to the office and see her family and friends. However, much to her surprise, after the second lockdown was announced she couldn't even pick up a paintbrush and the piano was pushed into the corner and covered up. For her, those two activities were associated with the lockdown and her struggles during that period. Another guest alleged that people struggled enough throughout the pandemic and once they came out of it they just wanted to move on and live an easier life again. Another guest said that some might feel a need to engage in new relationships and friendships rather than working on existing ones because it was easier to make a fresh start. People were dealing in different ways with COVID, the lockdowns, the uncertainties and isolation, and the loss of loved ones, sometimes more successfully than others.

Watching those programs made Sarah appreciate that everyone had struggled and had managed and faced the pandemic and the associated restrictions differently and in the best way they knew how. Most importantly, they were not alone in feeling trapped and hopeless.

Unlike George, Sarah kept herself fit. Come rain or shine, she went out for her daily walk. She only missed it for a single week when she contracted COVID. She made sure she connected or communicated with at least ten people a day, maybe over the phone, a nod or eye contact with someone she knew or a total stranger, on the street or through emails or text messages. For her, it was important to interact with people in any way legally allowed during that time. It was an important tool for keeping her sane. Sarah felt as though she dealt with lockdown better than George. Nevertheless, she did have her share of heartaches too.

Sarah's father died in 2021 during the time when the lockdown restrictions had been more or less lifted. Fortunately, her father had been persuaded by George's father Steve a long time ago to take out a good life insurance plan, so the funeral was paid for. But his passing had brought agonies to her life nonetheless. In addition to grieving for her father, because he hadn't established a will, deciding who should administer their father's estate became a bone of contention between Sarah and her brother, Tim.

When George and Sarah first met, Tim was a successful businessman operating a few restaurants in Edinburgh. So much so he was able to help with putting down a payment on the flat for their parents, which he gloated about countless times to Sarah's face.

Their mother had died about ten years ago and since then Tim had hit a string of bad luck resulting in him closing down a few restaurants. In part, this was due to bad management and also the excessive lifestyle he'd got accustomed to. He had two failed marriages behind him and in his late forties he was expecting a fifth child with his soon-to-be third wife.

Tim had been born prematurely, so ever since he was little their parents had pampered him with extra care and often allowed him to get away with not being accountable for his actions. They weren't wealthy by any means but they always somehow managed to comply with his demands to have the latest toys or the newest fashion accessories. Tim didn't get good qualifications from high school but to everyone's surprise, he graduated from a three-year college culinary course. For many years he worked for numerous restaurants after graduation and one day he told his parents that he wanted to run his own restaurant. He was never good with money, let alone saving any, so he persuaded his parents to loan him a sum, as silent business partners as he called it, to set up his first restaurant. The same investment deal was presented to Sarah but she turned it down because she knew it would not have been all plain sailing. For Sarah, from early on, she never wanted to have any financial dealings with him.

In the beginning, Tim worked hard and the restaurant was making a good profit so he opened a few more. On the surface, everything was in top shape with his lavish lifestyle and luxury cars. Tim acted and talked as if he was the king of the restaurateurs in Edinburgh.

"You should invest money in stocks and not just put it in the bank." Those patronising words from Tim still rang in Sarah's ears. She remembered a flashy ring Tim wore when he waved his hand laughing and generally lecturing her about her savings, not that there was much to begin with.

So it was much to Sarah's amazement when she discovered that on numerous occasions her brother had needed to borrow money from their parents to pay for various things, particularly his alimonies and child support after his divorces. She also later learned from her parents that they never received a penny back from Tim. Sarah felt particularly annoyed knowing that Tim kept taking advantage of their dad, especially as he just got by after the death of their mother. A few times her dad came asking for help because he had no money to give. In order not to put her dad in a difficult position Sarah and George gave cash to him for him to then give to Tim. They felt bad for Sarah's father but they also realised they had to halt coughing up money to fill an empty hole because the money they gave away was intended for their grandchildren.

In recent years Tim also took another financial hit trying to keep his last restaurants going, especially during the COVID lockdowns. Due to his lack of real understanding of finances and his other personal obligations Tim struggled, despite receiving financial support from the government. Much to her horror, Sarah also learned that her brother was in a legal battle with some of his staff for not paying out all the furlough support money he received.

After the death of their father, Tim thought that he should get a bigger slice of the proceeds because it was his money that made purchasing this flat possible, especially as the value had tripled in that area of Edinburgh since it was bought. On the other hand, from Sarah's point of view, the money Tim had put down for their parents' place had already been offset many times over by all the indefinable sums he'd borrowed here and there through the years.

Another event occurred that made Sarah even more insistent on getting a fair share of her father's estate. Before her father's passing, she was told by him there were about two thousand pounds in cash he had hidden in a plastic bag taped behind the TV in the living room. Later when she and her brother went to retrieve the bag there was only one thousand pounds found. Sarah hid her disappointment and suspicion from her brother but called Kimberly right away once she got home.

"I'm livid. I need to confront your uncle," stated Sarah with anger written all over her face. "I can't believe he would steal from his own father!"

"Mum, you don't know that. It could be that Granddad didn't remember the correct amount. There is no proof one way or the other. You have to let it go!" Kimberly said in a firm tone.

"OK... I see your point. Hey, don't tell your father. I don't want him to worry. Besides, you know how your father feels about your uncle. I don't want to create more friction between them. Your father often asks whether there is something he could help with concerning dealing with your uncle and sorting out your Granddad's estate, but after all, it's my brother and I prefer to deal with it alone."

"Mum's the word. I will not say anything to Dad. Call me after the mediation session. I'm sure you and Uncle Tim will find a solution."

A few days after her talk with Kimberly, Sarah attended a pro-bono mediation session with Tim but unfortunately failed to find a resolution or agreement on the estate. The case had escalated to a family court and the process was lengthy. Both she and Tim submitted applications for legal aid to meet the costs of legal advice and representation in court because they were not able to afford to hire a lawyer on their own.

Evidently, Sarah was devastated about it all and Kimberly could see how consumed with anxiety her mother had become since she and Tim had failed to settle.

"Mum, are you sure it will all be worth it?" Kimberly raised her question noticing how much it was weighing on Sarah. It was on the tip of her tongue to tell

Sarah that Tim and his children had unfriended her on Facebook but then grasped it would just add fuel to the fire.

"You know what, I'm not just doing this for my own peace of mind, but also because I want to protect what is rightfully yours and your children's!"

The process was long and the waiting between sessions was tedious. Sarah knew she was in for a long fight. While the court case was going on Sarah and Tim were not on talking terms and communicated only through their respective lawyers. She was dismayed to realise the possibility of losing contact with Tim and his children completely after the court case was over.

It was because of this therefore that she finally became supportive of George carrying on with researching more about Freya. She also then saw the value in George wanting to restore contact with Andrew.

*

"Are you still awake?" whispered George in the dark lying next to her.

"Erm, aye. What time is it?" mumbled Sarah in surprise. In her half-asleep state of mind, she wasn't aware George had come to bed.

"Oh, just after eleven. Guess what, I called Andrew and he agreed to meet me," said George with a loud yawn.

"How nice. I'm happy for you," she replied sleepily.

"I'm beat," sighed George.

"You…" Sarah halted. Initially, she wanted to advise George to be respectful and mindful this time with Andrew but she knew it certainly would not be well received. She was too tired to start a fight or an argument. "Never mind. Sleep well," said Sarah, who couldn't keep her eyelids open which made her realise how tired she was.

What will be will be was her last thought before she fell asleep.

Chapter 9 – 2022

Even though Andrew was pre-warned by Kimberly about George's call, he was nevertheless apprehensive about it. He didn't know what to expect but was intrigued when Kimberly mentioned in her message that George would like to ask him something about his father. *What did she mean?*

Andrew didn't have to wait long because George called that same evening. George went straight to the point about applying to the TV program.

"Wouldn't it be great? Me, finding more about my birth mother and you searching for your father? You have seen the program, haven't you?"

"Yes, I have. But—"

"Don't you think it would be a selling point for two cousins to be finding their lost relatives at the same time?" asked George, not hiding his enthusiasm.

"Let me think about it. Why don't we have an early dinner together this Saturday? It will give me a few days to think it over. Do you like Chinese food?"

"Aye, one of my favourites."

"Right. I'll send you details of the restaurant. I know the owner quite well and I am certain you would enjoy the food there. Five p.m.?" proposed Andrew.

"Great. Send me the address and I look forward to catching up."

Over the next couple of days, while mulling over the idea of finding his father, Andrew also spent time searching on the internet to find more about the TV program, what the application process entailed, and what to expect if one should be selected to take part. He had a few sleepless nights of anxiety but with a small flame of hope burning inside him, thinking *What if?*

That Saturday, Andrew went to the restaurant ahead of time in the afternoon. He was greeted by the owner Joey as soon as he stepped inside. They had a short chat before Joey led him to a table. While following behind him, Andrew was a little sombre and downcast when thinking about Joey's mother, Mama Evelyn, the original owner of the restaurant, and his own mother, both now passed away. After he sat down and glanced around the restaurant he then remembered with pleasure the friendship between the two families and how it had all begun.

*

Evelyn Wang and her husband along with their two boys, Joey and Jimi, immigrated from Hong Kong to Edinburgh in the mid-1970s.

The solid and long-lasting friendship between the Wang family and Andrew and his mother Hilary had begun when Evelyn first visited a corner shop near the Chinese takeaway she ran. The corner shop had been left to Hilary by her husband after he departed for New Zealand. Evelyn became a regular customer and the two women quickly developed a strong friendship. Eventually, Hilary sold her corner shop and came to work for Evelyn, first at the takeaway then later in the restaurant Evelyn opened up after the divorce from her husband. The two families went through thick and thin together and supported each other over the years. Family Wang's second son Jimi was the same age as Andrew and they grew up together and became inseparable at school and stood up for each other. They even came out at the same time in their mid-thirties and Jimi was self-proclaimed godfather to Andrew's son, Nathan. At one point Jimi moved to Spain with his husband and together they operated an exclusive B&B there but their bond with Andrew remained.

In his early twenties when Andrew worked for a real estate agency, he not only found the restaurant for Evelyn but also took charge of managing the renovation work for it which spurred an interest in becoming an interior designer.

Apart from his mum and his son, Mama Evelyn was also an invaluable person in Andrew's life. She had always been a surrogate mother figure to Andrew, and their friendship endured after Hilary died in 2010 when Andrew was forty-two.

During the first COVID lockdown, when people were not allowed to socialise or visit others, three or four times a week Andrew used to come by Evelyn's flat. He stood outside looking up and they were able to see each other. They waved at each other while talking on the phone.

Despite all the precautions Mama Evelyn contracted COVID and suffered complications due to other health issues. She died at eighty-two. As COVID restrictions eased towards the end of that lockdown, much to her joy in her final days, all her children and grandchildren came to Edinburgh. They as well as Andrew were at her bedside in the days before she passed away.

Andrew had been asked to give a talk about Mama Evelyn at the memorial service after the burial. Looking around the room, Andrew knew Evelyn was well-respected in the Asian community here in Scotland due to her tireless contributions to various charitable organisations and her involvement in the church. He was nevertheless amazed at how many people attended the memorial service to pay their respects.

He began his talk about their first encounter.

"'Call me Mama Evelyn'. I remember her saying that with a warm smile and patting my head when we first met." Andrew was choked up when he started his talk about the woman with whom he'd formed a friendship that lasted about half a century.

Andrew cleared his throat and continued, "She has been a vitally important figure to my family. She helped my mum to raise me, and my son. Mama Evelyn was like a second mother to me and an extra grandmother to my son. I'm forever grateful for her and her family's support throughout my life, especially during the loss of my own mother and… and my son." Andrew paused and took a glance at the pictures of Mama Evelyn placed around the room. They filled his heart with pride to have known this woman.

"The only time she was really angry with me was when she caught me and Jimi smoking when we were teenagers specially with Jimi because he was the one who provided me with the cigarettes." Andrew pointed at Jimi sitting on the front road.

Everyone laughed.

"She would want this occasion not to be sad, but rather to be a great party, a celebration of her life." Andrew continued on to deliver the last part of his speech making sure it was worthy and reflected the great woman she was.

*

Andrew was deep in thought contemplating visiting Mama Evelyn's and his mother's graves the next morning when Joey approached the table.

"Andrew, your guest has arrived."

Andrew looked up and saw George standing behind Joey. Joey and Andrew nodded at each other with a smile and Joey left.

"Hi, George. Have a seat." Andrew gestured with his hand and pointed at the chair across from him.

George reached out for an awkward handshake before he sat down.

"Nice place." Turning his head around, he admired the room. "You would not think it's a traditional Chinese

Restaurant. Very modern and… what is the word… oh yes, cosy. Must be the first time I've seen so many lanterns in such vibrant colours," admired George as he looked up at the ceiling.

"As it happens, I helped interior design the place many years back. I…" Andrew stopped and realised he wasn't comfortable sharing too much about himself and his relationship with the restaurant.

George didn't notice Andrew had cut short his explanation. He was busy studying the menu.

"I don't recognise any of these dishes. They don't look anything like my usual Chinese takeaway." George pointed at some of the photos and raised his head to look at Andrew for help.

"Yes, these are more authentic ones. I know the menu quite well, that is if you don't mind I'll order. Anything you don't eat?"

"I'm starving! So, anything and everything. Just nothing too spicy," revealed George. Just then his stomach happened to rumble.

They both chuckled and the underlying uneasiness between them faded somewhat.

During the dinner, George explained further to Andrew about his idea of applying to the TV show. He thought perhaps two cousins applying together might get more attention and make it more likely for the application to be accepted.

"Kimberly has already made the initial online application and received a comprehensive questionnaire to complete. I've asked Kimberly this morning to send you the questionnaire for you to look at. Have you got it?" asked George.

"Yes, we exchanged messages earlier today. In fact, this idea was suggested to me already a while ago by a friend of mine and it had always been in the back of my mind. Not going to lie, I'm now tempted but I'm in two minds about it. After all, my father left us for a reason and maybe he didn't want to be found," stated Andrew, shrugging his shoulders.

"Oh, I hadn't thought of that!" George was dumbfounded. He took off his glasses and polished them with the napkin, pondering Andrew's words.

"Another observation I have is that it's quite intrusive of one's privacy being on the show. I'm not sure I'm ready for that. Are you?" Andrew sounded genuinely concerned.

"Yes, Sarah and I discussed it. I just feel at this stage of my life I don't have anything to lose. Aileen said she would also help as much as she can to facilitate the search process, that is if I'm chosen."

"Righto. I'll read through the questionnaire and other requirements and get back to you in a week once I've had a chance to think about it properly," suggested Andrew.

The two cousins had a pleasant meal together though both never fully let their guard down. However, George was nevertheless pleased that the meeting went better than he'd anticipated. Carrying a bag of takeaway Andrew had ordered for Sarah, George was beaming to himself and feeling hopeful when he walked out of the restaurant heading home.

Andrew stayed a little longer and left the restaurant just after eight p.m. Once he exited the door he was met with misty air. He walked alongside Princes Street heading back towards the West End. He saw that a few people were still out and about. Something drew Andrew's attention and he looked up to his left and saw a full moon shining above Edinburgh Castle, which proudly stood upon the plug of an extinct volcano in the middle of the city. It was almost mystical. It never failed to amaze him how stunning the castle was each time he saw it. Usually, it would fill him with a sense of calm and stability, except that evening Andrew felt nothing but drained. Talking to George had brought back all his old struggles of abandonment and anger towards his father. On the one hand, he would like to know how his father was doing but was also afraid of rejection again and learning the reason why he had left them. Andrew kept his head down, walking. He was deeply absorbed in thought when, out of nowhere, from the corner of his eye he saw someone rapidly approaching him apparently trying to communicate with him.

Andrew jumped and almost let go of the bag he was carrying. His body tensed. "I don't have any money," declared Andrew, out of reflex.

"I'm not asking for money! I'm just hungry," pleaded the man in front of him.

Taking a closer look Andrew saw a young man with something genuine in his eyes. He stopped. As Andrew hadn't moved on, the young man started telling him his story. He had come up to Edinburgh from Manchester to live and work for his estranged father. They had a falling out which left him homeless and he had no money to go back home to Manchester.

After listening to the young man's story his heart softened. *No wonder he's standing outside McDonald's.* "OK. How about I buy you something to eat?" Andrew offered.

They went in and Andrew ordered two portions of food for Matthew, the name the young man introduced himself by. Without a care in the world, Matthew enjoyed eating the burger and fries with a satisfied smile on his face. While Matthew was wolfing down the food, across from him Andrew smelled a distinctive body odour from him. It was a smell of dampness mixed with urine and sweat. A sudden idea entered Andrew's head. Maybe he should offer him a place to stay for the night or even just to wash his clothes or take a shower. Another thought quickly arose that he had been daft to even think about it.

"Thanks for the dinner! I'll keep one for tomorrow. I've got to hurry back to the shelter for the night. My mum promised to send some money so I can travel home in a few days," said Matthew. He removed the plastic cap of the cup and finished his drink. He cleared the table and carefully put one burger into a paper bag then tucked it in his rucksack.

They went out of McDonald's and Matthew said his goodbye with a firm handshake. Andrew stood still for a few moments then realised he should have offered money to Matthew but he had already walked away and disappeared in the dark. *I should have given my email address for him to contact me in case he needs help.*

Suddenly Andrew was hit by a realisation that the reason he was drawn to Matthew was because he was about the same age as Nathan when he died. His heart ached. Nathan died sixteen years ago but thinking about anything that remotely reminded him of his son and his death still hurt.

When he got home, even before he took off his coat, he instinctively called Jimi in Spain to tell him about his encounters that day.

"You wanted to do what? Honestly, you must be joking thinking about offering him to come and stay in your place. Imagine the headline in the news tomorrow. A gay man on the verge of passing his best before date lured a young man to his home for some scandalous and dodgy activities..." teased Jimi and wasn't able to continue as he was laughing so hard at his own joke he had to gasp for air and nearly dropped his phone. Occasionally, as a reflection of the strength of their solid friendship, they both enjoyed throwing each other under the bus, so to speak.

"Ha-ha. Hilarious. I mean, I just wanted to help him. He seemed so helpless." Scratching his head, Andrew innocently defended his action with naïve eagerness, like a child in front of a teacher or parents. "I—"

Jimi barged in. "Hey! On a serious note, I know you want to be nice but you also have to be careful."

Andrew paused and chewed over Jimi's words, which he could see the sense of, but the young man had reminded him so much of Nathan.

Jimi interpreted Andrew's silence as uncertainty and continued to expand on his reasoning.

"Don't remember if I told you what happened to me during lockdown? When restrictions were easing up I was walking home one afternoon after I'd finished a volunteer shift preparing meals for homeless people in a rough area of the town. I saw two teenage girls dressed somewhat provocatively walking in front of me down a narrow alley. At that time the social distancing requirement was still strongly recommended so I paid extra attention, walking behind and trying not to be too close to them. They walked, I walked. They stopped, I stopped till one of the girls turned and challenged me in an angry high-pitched voice and asked whether I was following them," Jimi said in an annoyed tone.

"Maybe they really felt uncomfortable thinking you were in fact following them?"

"They wish. Well, I guess…" Jimi's voice weakened and then faded away while he chewed over the possibility of a misunderstanding that he hadn't been aware of.

"So what did you say to them?" Andrew curiously put forward his question while he tilted his shoulder to one side and used one hand to take off his coat and walked to the living room.

"Nothing! What could I say? I'm a mature Asian man and they were two teenage girls. Whatever I said would be interpreted wrongly. Imagine if they started screaming?" Jimi said with a sigh.

"And?"

"I ignored them and just walked past them. I kept walking without looking back. Knowing me, guess what I actually wanted to say to them?"

"Don't know. Go on, amuse me."

"What I wanted to say to them was that my standards are extremely low but I do have standards," joked Jimi with a sarcastic laugh.

"Man, that joke never gets old!" Andrew exclaimed with a grin on his face. He felt somewhat less heavy-hearted.

"Seriously, you have to protect yourself, especially nowadays," Jimi insisted, trying to make Andrew understand the possible implications of the issue.

"I know. Appreciate the talk. By the way, how are you doing with recovering from COVID?" asked Andrew, changing the subject.

"It was scary at first when I saw two lines appear on the testing kit last week but since I already got three vaccines the symptoms were mild. I was in bed for two days then I was fine. I tested this morning and I am negative."

"Great to know." Andrew yawned. "I'm beyond tired. I know, old age, as you would say. I'll call you in a few days to tell you about my conversation with my cousin George."

"OK! See you in five weeks anyway. Thank god no more quarantines are needed though I'm still in two minds about wearing a facial covering during the flight or not."

"I would! See you then. I'll get the guest bedroom ready."

After their call, Andrew fell on the sofa in the dark. He thought about Jimi's upcoming trip back to Edinburgh with his husband to attend a ceremony to mark the one-year anniversary of his mother's death. *Has it been one year already?*

Talking to Jimi, especially after his cheeky jokes, often cheered him up but they had many deep and difficult discussions too. They were only able to be vulnerable in front of each other because of their profound friendship rooted in trust and respect. But this evening Andrew felt unbearably exhausted. He massaged his temples to ease the tightness but was overwhelmed by thousands of thoughts running through his head.

Growing up without a father, Andrew was not unfamiliar with being bullied and was not a stranger to name-calling about him and his mother. As for Jimi and his family, living in Scotland in the seventies, they experienced many times verbal abuse with racial slurs, including people making fun of their last name or purposely mispronouncing it. More recently, when the pandemic first became known and started spreading, Jimi and his friends were leaving a restaurant one day when he was targeted by a few youngsters. "Here comes the COVID!" they shouted mockingly at Jimi's group before running off with ear-splitting laughs.

Ever since Andrew had known Jimi and his family they had always committed with sweat and tears to tirelessly working long hours, first in the takeaway and then in the restaurant. Jimi put a lot of effort into his studies and progressing in his career. He earned himself a well-respect position at the United Nations in Geneva where he worked for many years before moving to Spain, but more than once he heard comments about his achievements that he just tried to be *White*.

"I don't even know what that means. Just because I worked hard and wanted to achieve something in my life I'm being labelled as wanting to be White? Does it mean all non-white people can't or don't deserve to succeed?" contested Jimi, rolling his eyes. Andrew found himself tongue-tied when Jimi had told him that a few such remarks and comments had come from Andrew's gay acquaintances.

"It's impossible! How could gay people be racist?" Andrew was stunned and visibly appalled by what he heard. He paused a bit to mull over this thought before explaining his confusion. "I just thought people would be more mindful and compassionate, especially those who've experienced hardships and judgement themselves."

"Yes, naively I thought so too at first but the truth is that racism exists in every group and sub-group. Human nature is complex. Unfortunately, just because you're gay or from a minority group, like all humans, does not exempt, prevent or even immunise you from being racist or having any prejudices or discrimination towards others. I read once an article about how in social settings humans often tactically single out the weakest, aiming to avoid being identified as one," explained Jimi.

Laying on the sofa with the previous conversations he'd had with Jimi circulating in his head, Andrew fell asleep. At one point he shivered and woke up. He turned his head and noticed a wall-mounted digital clock displaying 1.22 a.m. *Better get up before I catch a cold.* He finally headed to the bathroom to get ready for bed.

That night Andrew tossed and turned. His head was full of emotion and thoughts of the three people who were no longer in his life. Two had given him his life, and the other he'd brought into this life. His mother died twelve years ago; his father had left without a trace when he was a toddler. The last one was his son Nathan, who he'd buried at age nineteen after the car accident.

Thinking about them, Andrew couldn't help feeling totally dejected and overwhelmingly sad. He closed his eyes, attempting to fall asleep but failing. He sensed a pressure on his bladder, an urge to pee, but stubbornly remained in his bed. Then he heard that disturbing sound of the combi-boiler turning on. *For God's sake!* Finally, his bladder won, he wasn't able to hold it in any longer. He pulled away the duvet and was hit by a sudden chill. He shivered, so he quickly put on his bathrobe and dragged himself to the bathroom.

"Phew." He felt his shoulders sag.

While washing his hands, he contemplated what would be the least hassle to prepare in the kitchen. Andrew then walked to the kitchen and fetched milk and honey from the fridge and a saucepan but then put them back. *Can't be bothered to brush my teeth again.* Instead, he put the kettle on. After he'd made his hot drink, he walked back and sat up on the bed. While finishing his cup of chamomile tea, he turned on his phone and peeked at the display. *3.54 a.m.!* He put on an episode of his favourite program, Judy Justice, and placed the phone on the bedside table. He knew it was a bad habit but at times it had helped him to fall asleep in the past. It was a trick he'd discovered during the COVID lockdown when he suffered from insomnia. As he turned the volume quite low, his over-loaded thoughts were distracted by him having to focus his full concentration on listening. Halfway through the episode he fell asleep, though not soundly.

He dreamt about his mother. In the dream, Andrew was calling her but struggled to get hold of her. Either he dialled an incorrect number or his fingers were too feeble to press the dialling pad. The more he tried, the more his frustration intensified because he wasn't able to speak to her.

Chapter 10 – 2022

The next morning Andrew woke up heavy-headed and was baffled by the dream. It had been quite a while since his mum had appeared in his dreams. Right after his mother died, after the funeral when everything went back to 'normal' again, Andrew wasn't able to talk about her, and he was even afraid to dream about her. He just wasn't ready to face the fact that she was no longer alive. Then he eventually did start to dream about her, either they were supposed to meet up but kept missing each other or for whatever reason they were unable to communicate despite standing in front of each other. A few times in the dream he called out "Mum!" and was woken up by his own shouting.

Andrew dragged his feet and sluggishly walked to the bathroom. He felt refreshed as soon as he took a shower but as he wiped off the steam on the mirror he saw a tired face with puffy eyes looking back at him. *YUCK! Not a pretty sight. Not a pretty sight at all.* Andrew could imagine how Jimi would mock him, which brought a cheeky grin to his face. He started feeling more upbeat. He opened his medicine cabinet and took out his shaving kit.

Drips.

Oh, a damn nosebleed! Andrew reached and got hold of a piece of toilet paper and pressed it under his nose. As he looked up he realised it wasn't a nosebleed, rather he had cut himself shaving. Blood blended with the shaving foam and a few drops escaped and dripped down. Andrew carefully wiped off the reddish mixture of shaving foam and blood and saw a smooth, clean incision in the skin. It hurt and stung more than Andrew had anticipated from such an insignificant cut.

Andrew put pressure on the area with a tissue to stop the bleeding while he reflected on his talk with George and then his mind switched to the encounter he'd had with the young guy Matthew outside the McDonald's last night. Instantaneously, he was hit with unfathomable sorrow as Matthew reminded him once again of his son Nathan. It has been sixteen years since Nathan's death and there wasn't a day that went by without Andrew thinking about him. He could still remember the first time he'd held him right after he was born, the agonising moment he was told about his death and the day he was handed Nathan's ashes in an urn. He couldn't help wondering if Nathan were still alive would he have a family of his own? He was gripped by a heart-rending sensation and became choked up with grief.

Though Andrew was not aware of it, his emotional outbreak that morning was about far more than just missing his mother and his son. Repressed emotions buried during the lockdowns had surfaced as well. The time spent alone in total isolation with never-ending days trying to make up chores to make sense of each day had affected him. At times he felt isolated and invisible and forgotten by the world. After the final lockdown was eased, he experienced anxiety and distress when he had to interact with people and with society again.

My goodness. I better pull myself together otherwise nothing will be done today.

With that pep talk to himself, Andrew got dressed. Although it was a Sunday he sat in his home office and sent a few work-related messages. Lunchtime came and he went to the kitchen and put the kettle on. While waiting for the water to boil he thought about his friend Tom and about how their friendship had evolved. It took time for Tom to let anyone into his life but with time they became good friends and had grown closer during lockdown. Tom was one of the very few people Andrew met face to face during restrictions when it was permitted.

Despite Tom having published two novels, with one even being turned into a motion picture, he was literally one of the most down-to-earth people Andrew had met. Tom never bragged about his achievements or viewed himself as successful or famous. He remained humble and lived as ordinary a life as possible.

"After the novels and film were released and all the fuss calmed down I went back to being myself again, Mr Nobody. I'm glad that I'm not included in any of these so-called celebrity circles or in environments where I know I don't belong. I don't care if people consider me to be dull but I'd rather be disliked for who I am rather than liked for who I am not." Tom's words rang now in Andrew's ears.

When they'd first met, Andrew did find Tom a bit passive and cautious. Andrew saw him having difficulties in expressing his true emotions and that said a lot coming from Andrew. As they got to know each other better, Andrew understood they got on because they had many similarities; both suffered from fear of abandonment. Tom had had a challenging childhood, to say the least, not knowing his mother and his father not being much involved in his life. He was raised by his paternal grandparents. His mother died right after giving birth to him and his father was already married and had a family of his own. Due to his family background and upbringing, he had a lifelong quest for validation but only learnt that it didn't mean anything unless one valued oneself. After the later death of his father and through his writing journey he'd come to terms with finding forgiveness and had let go of the anger towards his father.

From thinking of Tom, Andrew couldn't help comparing him with his other friend Jimi. Tom was a good example of an introvert, the total opposite of Jimi. Andrew had a twinkle in his eyes when he thought about his two closest friends and when he had introduced them during lockdown. Andrew, Tom and Jimi had regular Zoom calls to support each other. During one of these calls, Jimi told Andrew to start dating again and discovered that Tom was also longing to find a girlfriend. Both of them were out of touch and rusty in the dating scene.

"You should try using apps. Believe you me, you will find them intriguing," suggested Jimi, rather encouragingly.

Jimi then explained to them how those apps worked and the dos and don'ts. It was as though a new world opened up for them once they were comfortable with the idea. Jimi took charge of setting up and creating their profiles and uploading their photos.

One day Jimi called for a chat.

"Tom and I now call you our online dating pimp," mocked Andrew. "Take it as a term of endearment."

"Charming!" From the sound of his reply, Jimi had happily accepted the title.

"You're welcome!"

"By the way, thanks for checking in on my mum. I will come to Edinburgh as soon as the goddamn travel restrictions are over! Any success with the apps?"

"If you told me a few months ago I would be using dating apps and enjoying them I would never have believed you. Speaking for Tom, I understand he feels the same way and I think he's getting the hang of it. For me, chatting with guys even though we're not able to meet up face to face helps me not go insane from total isolation! So, thanks," Andrew expressed his gratitude to Jimi for convincing him to overcome his fear of joining the online scene.

"I told you! So have you chatted with any interesting profiles?" Jimi was curious.

"Yes, the other day I met up with a guy I'd chatted with for a walk along the Water of Leith. When no one was around, I handed him a razor and asked him to shave the back of my neck—"

"Come again! You asked him to do *what*?" Jimi cut in. He leapt up quickly in surprise, almost knocking over the chair. He thought that he must have misheard what Andrew just told him.

"Well, we're not allowed to go to the barbers and they're all shut anyway! My hair grew too long on the back of my neck so I asked him to shave it off for me. It was the most intimate moment I'd had for a long time!" Andrew defended himself as best he could.

"Err, OK. Then?" Jimi was now intrigued, holding his breath in suspense.

"Nothing. Then we went our separate ways after the walk. We were not allowed to invite each other home because we're from different households, remember!"

"No way! Oh, Andy boy. You're hopeless! Guys are on those dating apps to find hook-ups and you chatted up someone to shave your neck. Each to his own, I suppose, each to his own."

Lockdown was hard emotionally and psychologically but the three of them as well as Jimi's husband had promised each other not to buy a dog out of boredom. During one of their calls, Tom had mentioned that he'd put on a few extra pounds which prompted them all to exercise and stay fit, despite being in this difficult period. They also made a pact vowing not to eat after six p.m.

At first, Andrew thought it would be a good idea to invite George to join their group chat but then he decided against contacting him because George had just lost his father, who had died in the care home. Plus, he wasn't sure if George would have the right mindset for it at that time. He might perhaps even see it as an insult or an intrusion. After all, Jimi and Tom were his friends whom he'd known for many years. In Andrew's mind he came to realise that dealing with relatives could be much trickier and less straightforward.

"One can't prevent wrinkles but there is no excuse for putting on weight," said Jimi, rolling his eyes while at the same time pointing at his firm and flat stomach.

"Impressive," Tom praised.

"I'm going blind, I'm going blind!" Andrew chuckled as he saw on his screen Jimi sounding and acting just like his mother, Mama Evelyn.

Jimi was never short of ideas. After a while, he even started and led a group on a social media platform organising talks about diet, daily exercise and mental health to encourage and support others who were struggling with lockdown restrictions. It was thanks to this group that Andrew felt at his best physically and gained a nice body tone that he'd never had before as an adult. This group continued and became a regular weekly event even after all the COVID restrictions were lifted. A legacy of the pandemic that they were proud of.

Just as Andrew was lingering over thoughts of Jimi and Tom and their struggles during the COVID restrictions his phone suddenly rang. It gave him a fright but it also jolted him back to the present moment. He took a quick glance at the screen and pressed to answer it right away.

"How spooky is that! I was just thinking of calling you later today. What's up?" he asked Tom.

"Oh, nothing special. Just thought you might want to meet for lunch one day next week? There are a few new restaurants opened up in the St James Quarter," suggested Tom.

"Aye, that would be nice. What about Wednesday at one p.m.? We can decide later where to meet up."

"Grand. You mentioned you wanted to call me. Anything special on your mind?"

"Yes. I met my cousin for dinner yesterday and he proposed that we contact a TV show helping people find their lost relatives. His mother died when he was little so he would like to know whether he still has relatives from her side. In my case to find my father. What do you think?"

"Oh, interesting. I've seen that show on TV but how does it work?" asked Tom, intrigued.

"So, my cousin's daughter already made the initial application online and received an induction pack with questionnaires to fill in and that is where I have some problems with it," explained Andrew.

Andrew went on to outline his doubts to Tom. He explained that initially, he'd been excited but at the same time frightened about the potential intrusiveness into his privacy. Meanwhile, he had great anxiety over what the TV program may or may not find out about his father.

"What if he had another family and doesn't want to know anything about me? Or what if he's dead?" Andrew shared his worries with Tom.

Tom was quiet, contemplating, but before he was able to answer, Andrew continued. "I really don't like to share anything about Nathan's death with the public, which I'm sure will be brought up somehow. For me, it's a very personal and private thing. Yes, your second novel was loosely based on my life and readers of yours may or may not associate my life with your novel so at least I can mostly remain anonymous on that front. I'm afraid being on TV will change that."

"I see what you mean," replied Tom. "Do you remember that incident that happened to me on social media in 2020?"

*

Tom's second novel was released just a few months before COVID arrived in Scotland. He participated in only a few carefully selected interviews with radio, magazines and newspapers prior to the lockdown. He was extra careful because he'd already been through bad experiences with it before, after his first novel had been released. Nevertheless, in order to further promote the novel, he then agreed with the publisher to arrange a handful of virtual interviews as well.

During one of the interviews, just before it ended, the interviewer talked about the Clap for Our Carers movement and expressed the idea that it was an opportunity to open the windows to get some fresh air as well. Tom was very involved in this social moment, which was created as a gesture of appreciation for the workers of the UK's National Health Service and other key workers during the pandemic. At eight p.m. every Thursday people leaned out of their windows and all clapped together, applauding the efforts of the care workers.

Tom expressed his respect for all the UK health service staff and other key workers. He said that he hoped one day we wouldn't need to thank them any more for just doing their job because they had been so well-respected and were provided with the correct personal protection equipment as well as being financially compensated for the vital work they were doing, especially during the COVID.

The interviewer thanked Tom for his time and the interview ended and Tom didn't think much about it. However, he found out a few days later that a small headline in the online magazine read – **Author Tom Gibbs does not think we need to thank the NHS workers.**

Tom was so mortified he wasn't able to finish reading it further after he saw the headline and he was worried that people would do exactly the same, just focus on the headline. The fact of the matter was if one read the whole interview it clearly stated how much Tom appreciated the NHS and their contributions and sacrifices, especially during the pandemic.

Sure enough, Tom received a backlash of critical comments. There were also those who defended him after they had read the full interview, and the whole thing resulted in much debate on social media, which led in turn to discussion about him and his novels. Although Tom had agreed to the interview because he understood that exposure was needed to promote his novels, he had never anticipated this kind of controversial attention, especially since it did not help to increase book sales. The truth was that those who were involved in the debate were not necessarily his readers and did not rush to order the book.

"I've never understood the saying '*there is no such thing as bad publicity*'," opined Tom raising his voice as he expressed his dismay to his publisher. "Can you imagine that my name will be forever linked to the headline of this interview in future Google searches!"

After the heat caused by the troublesome interview had died down, Tom became even more reluctant about any dealings with the media, especially social media.

*

"I really can't advise you what to do, whether it's the right decision for you to be on TV or not. My bad experience with the media doesn't mean it will happen to you too," Tom pointed out.

Before they ended their call Tom asked Andrew not to make any hasty decisions. He also told Andrew to forward him those online questionnaires and promised that he'd find out more about the process before their lunch appointment.

After a week was up, Andrew received a call from George keenly asking him whether or not he had made his decision.

"Sorry, George. I still need more time to think about it. It's not an easy decision to make. Hope you understand," explained Andrew.

Andrew had carefully read through the questionnaires along with Tom and Jimi and all three of them agreed that the terms and conditions were eloquent if not too forceful. They felt that it would be necessary to reveal quite a lot of personal and family information which Andrew ultimately wasn't prepared to share.

Once Andrew had made up his mind, he called George to inform him about his decision but before he was able to explain his reason, George cut him off. Blood rushed to George's head as his face turned red. Words lashed out of his mouth faster than he was able to think. He lost his temper as his anger got the better of him. George totally misinterpreted Andrew's decision as if it was a personal rejection. Feeling already inadequate because of his previous behaviour, he took it as a direct insult towards him.

Sarah was in the living room when she suddenly heard George raising his voice but when she figured it out what it was about, it was too late to stop him. She rushed to the kitchen and heard George expressing his anger and disappointment. He shouted at Andrew and told him he'd wasted his time and before Andrew had a chance to reply he hung up.

"What did you do?" Sarah was appalled, to put it lightly. She wasn't able to think of a reason why George had acted so angrily towards Andrew.

"He said he won't take part in the search project. After all this time! He led me on and now he said he won't take part!" sulked George. Underneath it all was the bitter disappointment that he wouldn't be able to build bridges and bond with Andrew over the show after all. Though he was unable to admit it to Sarah at that moment, deep down he quickly realised the further damage he had done to the relationship between him and Andrew.

"Yes it's unfortunate he made that decision but you can't force him. He has his reasons and he's entitled to do whatever he wants. It's his prerogative to make whatever choice suits him. Andrew does not owe you anything. You might be disappointed but you can't take it out on him." It took Sarah a great deal of effort to reason with George.

"Don't you think the TV program would be interested to do an episode about the two cousins, one to find out about his mother's relatives in Germany and one to find out about his father in New Zealand? Anyway, forget about it. I'll continue with just me then," grumbled George, still not backing down despite the realisation he had overreacted.

"You're impossible! You shouldn't burn the bridges with your cousin, your only cousin!" warned Sarah, worried about the possible consequence of his bad temper.

"But—"

"There is no but about it! Call back or send a message to apologise," without hesitation, Sarah cut George off with her order.

"Fine. I... I... just give me a moment!" argued George.

"You're impossible!" Sarah repeated and these were her last words before she slammed the door behind her in frustration. She was infuriated with her husband and thought it best for her to take a walk to avoid further arguments or having to listen to his excuses. Truth be told, she wasn't able to look at him right then.

George sat alone in the kitchen after Sarah had stormed out of their home. He was fuming and felt rather sorry for himself. His initial reaction was that he wanted to prove how wrong Andrew was in not taking part. After a while, he became bored with his own sulking so he went through the fridge and kitchen cupboards searching for something to eat. He grabbed a can of Coke but then at the last moment, he put it back and grabbed a banana instead. After he closed one cupboard door he saw the photo of Freya which he had framed and hung nearby. For a reason he couldn't explain, he failed to meet her eyes as though she was looking at him with great disappointment.

What's going on?

He sat down, peeled the banana and was about to eat it when he felt Freya's eyes staring at him. He changed seats but somehow he sensed that Freya's disapproving gaze followed him and he wasn't able to shake off an uncomfortable feeling of shame with a burning sensation on his face. Unnerved, he escaped the kitchen and went to the bathroom. He turned the tap on and splashed his face with cold water. As he raised his head he avoided meeting his own eyes in the mirror. He then dragged his feet to the living room. He blew out a long breath after he sat down on the sofa. He thought of calling Kimberly or Aileen but instead, he sat there in silence. It was only then that he finally calmed down and wondered why he had imagined Freya was staring at him.

Would she be disappointed in me? This thought led him to reflect on his previous discussions with Sarah. He himself would be the last person to let himself be forced into doing something against his will, so why would he have expected anything different from Andrew?

But, imagine how happy Andrew would be if he found his father. Another thought entered his mind that it was not his place to determine what would be happy or not for others. *Why do I often put myself in this kind of position? Why can't I think before I lash out?*

Eventually, he registered the depth of his own stupidity and how he had acted unfairly towards Andrew. It was not his place to pressure him. He wanted to call to apologise but was too afraid of the humiliation if Andrew were to reject it. Finally, George did send a message of apology and it was acknowledged as 'Read' but no further replies came from Andrew. Staring at his phone, George felt extremely low and longed for someone to talk to. He finally called Kimberly and told her what had happened.

"Why did… Oh, never mind. Don't call him or send more texts. Let things cool down for a while," suggested Kimberly, knowing there was no point putting more blame on her father.

"I guess…"

In the days that followed, Kimberly helped George to complete the questionnaire, indicating all the relevant timelines and they submitted all the requested documents and photos with the help of Aileen.

They waited for about six weeks before someone from the production team contacted them to inform them that they were keen on this search if they wished to go further with an initial interview.

Sarah and Kimberly were happy for George, but they made it clear to him that he still needed to think through all the implications before signing any contract with the TV program even if the interview went well.

For George, he didn't care about any of that at that point. So many things had happened in his life in the past two and half years with COVID, the death of his father, problems at work and the discovery of the photos of Freya and Tomer. At that moment he really needed something positive to happen in his life, and his mind was totally focused on the search for his relatives without weighing up the possible consequences of the outcome, whatever they might be.

Chapter 11 – 2022/2023

Right after George signed the contract with the TV program, he phoned Aileen in California. She had left Scotland in the late summer of 2022 for a long stay with Alistair's family once she finished helping George with the submission of the application.

It just so happened that when he phoned, all Alistair's children and grandchildren had come to visit and that prevented them from having as long a conversation as George had anticipated. He knew it was childish but George was full of envy and a feeling of being left out of all the laughter in the background when Aileen apologetically told him to call back the day after.

"She's now with her real family," George moaned to Sarah about his shortened conversation with Aileen.

"You can't think like that!" Sarah pointed out when she sensed the frustration in George's tone.

George bit his lip not daring to say a word but with disappointment showing all over his face.

"You should be happy for Aileen and Alistair. Besides, the weather is better over there and it would be good for her health," placated Sarah.

"I suppose…"

"Focus on your own adventure! Think what exciting things the TV filming might find!"

Sarah was right. George was occupied with various requests from the TV people. He had to hand over original copies of the relevant photos and birth, death and marriage certificates that he'd obtained from the registrar's office of the City of Edinburgh Council. He was also requested to submit a sample of his DNA. Since then he and Sarah have had regular update calls with the TV program's producer and the first filming was scheduled to take place a few weeks after the interview followed by the signing of the contract.

George was fired with hope. He had never imagined being involved and engaged in such a project in his life. He took every opportunity to share it with everyone he knew about it, including people he met when he was working in a local charity. George had started volunteer work again on the recommendation of Sarah and Kimberly for the benefit of his mental well-being.

One Saturday while he was doing his shift, during the break he talked to a new male volunteer about the opportunity to take part in the TV program. As they'd never met before, George also took this opportunity to tell the man about his good intentions in wanting his cousin to take part and what a pity it was that his cousin decided not to get on board in the end. In George's mind, he wasn't complaining about Andrew or criticising him in his telling of the tale, rather he thought he was expressing how much of a shame it was that Andrew had missed the opportunity.

The man patiently listened to George without interrupting.

George took a quick glance at him but couldn't tell what he was thinking.

"Well, first I'm so pleased for you about the search and you being involved in the TV program. It sounds really interesting! But…" he paused to choose his words carefully before continuing, "do you mind if I share with you my tuppence worth?"

"Of course," replied George with a nod but sounding less than convinced. *What did I do wrong, or did I say something offensive?*

"You're obviously here because you're an empathetic person and have compassion about the cause and people you're helping. Why don't you feel the same about your cousin? I fully get your point about being frustrated that he changed his mind at the last minute but carrying this negative energy, being angry at him must wear you down? To forgive is the best gift to yourself. I'm not trying to lecture you. No doubt I'd find it difficult to let something like that go as well," stated the man with a kind light in his eyes, looking at George.

Though the man was soft-spoken and had responded to George in a non-intrusive manner, each of his words hit George so profoundly that it left him speechless for the rest of the shift. Something new awoke within George that even without directly saying anything negative about Andrew others perceived his attitude differently. He was stunned that someone else was able to detect his mixed sentiments towards Andrew. This made him rather uncomfortable but he was willing to give thought to the possibility. *I thought I wasn't angry with him any longer but I guess I still am.*

He recalled what Sarah had said about him, that he couldn't hide his likes and dislikes. His emotions were often written all over his face. It was then that he became aware that at times unspoken words could be even more telling and revealing and have real consequences as well. He felt that a light bulb had been switched on in his head at that moment.

"Are you OK? You seem a bit off this evening. Anything happen today at the volunteer place?" asked Sarah when she realised George was vacantly staring into space and pushing the food around his plate without eating it.

"No. Nothing special. I'm just a bit tired," he replied vaguely.

That evening George slept exceptionally well through the whole night without needing any sleeping aid. He was not the only beneficiary. Sarah also had a good night's sleep, not being disturbed by his usual loud snores.

In the following days, while waiting for any developments from the TV production team, George started doing his own research about his German and Jewish roots with the help of Sarah. They learned about a special upcoming celebration in Germany about Saint Nicholas. So, a few days later he called Kimberly and his grandchildren to share with them what he'd found out about this tradition.

On the night of the 5th of December, he put the shoes of their grandchildren next to an electric fireplace and sent a photo of it to them. The next morning, he sent another photo with their shoes full of small presents, which he and Sarah had bought, with a message indicating they were treats from Saint Nicholas. Their grandchildren were very excited about this new tradition and couldn't wait for those treats when they came to visit during the Christmas break.

George was so excited he also phoned Aileen to inform her about this new tradition and the grandkids' reaction.

"How wonderful!" remarked Aileen, sounding pleased for George.

"Mum, you're so lucky to have escaped the heavy snow we're having," exclaimed George, referring to the blizzards they had that December in 2022. "I don't remember ever seeing so much snow in Scotland!"

"Yes, I saw it on the news," she replied, "that thousands are without power after the snowstorm."

"We had the coldest night of the year last Sunday. Temperatures plummeted to below minus fifteen degrees in some places. Can you believe it? There is a lot of travel disruption across the country, and trains and fights are being delayed and cancelled everywhere," George reported.

"How terrible! Oh dear, oh dear! And how can people afford to heat their homes with the energy prices increasing so much recently!" remarked Aileen with worry in her tone.

"Believe it or not, there were some out-of-touch ministers that had the nerve to tell people to stop complaining and just put on more clothes to keep warm. Unbelievable!"

"People really have enough to deal with! What a few years we've had, and it's getting worse by the look of it!" Aileen sighed, referring to the aftermath of Brexit, COVID-19, instabilities within the government, the passing away of the Queen, inflation, price rises for energy and strikes in many sectors, including among NHS workers.

"I know. Oh, on a more cheerful note, Kimberly's children were beside themselves with joy playing in the snow. Also, they were thrilled about the closure of the schools of course," said George with a laugh.

Aileen laughed along.

"How are you doing, Mum? Do you like it over there or want to come home?"

"Not going to lie, it took a bit of time to adjust but I really like the warmer weather here. Alistair is busy managing and growing their vineyard, with help from Michelle. Their children and grandchildren come to visit often. It's a different lifestyle from Edinburgh that's for sure!" declared Aileen.

"That's nice. Tell them we say hello," said George, hoping his sincerity was noticeable.

"How are you doing anyway?"

"I…" George couldn't finish his sentence, weighing up whether he should tell Aileen about a recent unpleasant ordeal with a strange tightness in his chest, a sensation unlike the heartburn caused by indigestion or acid reflux he had experienced before. Sarah had nagged him to see his GP but he put it off, telling her it was most likely caused by the unusual weather conditions.

"George, are you there? How is the search going with the TV program?" For a moment Aileen thought she'd lost the connection as George had lapsed into silence.

"I'm here. Except for my bank card password, I think I've submitted everything," joked George with a sigh. "The little TV crew already came once last week and recorded me explaining the reason for my search."

"Were you nervous?"

"A bit. I was more worried about it being over-dramatic and sensationalised."

"What do you mean?"

"It was filmed when I went to Freya's grave and told my story standing in front of it. Though I don't know how much of it will be used in the final cut."

"Will they show it to you before it's aired on TV?" queried Aileen.

"I think so..." said George, not sounding convinced. "I've got to look at the contract that I signed with them. There were so many clauses and complicated legal jargon and terms I didn't understand."

"Make sure to ask the next time you talk to them."

"I will. Oh, thanks for your help with locating Freya's grave. In the end, you knew more than all of us! I would be lost without your help."

"Luckily, your dad told me about the cemetery once. As you are aware, your dad didn't talk much about the past unless I specifically asked him," she added.

"Your input was invaluable, really!"

They ended their call by chatting about the new traditions George wanted to explore. As George and Sarah went further with their own research, they wanted to pay respect to Freya so they were looking to have their first ever Hanukkah to celebrate the Festival of Lights. Sarah took up the challenge of making dinner for them during the celebration. She studied recipes and watched YouTube clips on how to make potato latkes, brisket with mushroom and onion gravy. She insisted on making her own braided egg-bread and went to stores that sold proper ingredients appropriate for this occasion.

When the time came, Kimberly and her family came down and they all celebrated their first Hanukkah together. Kimberly's children were too young to understand or appreciate the significance of this tradition so Sarah asked George to buy a Christmas tree as well so the kids could find their Christmas gifts under it like the previous years.

George valued very much Sarah's effort in making this occasion special because he'd never practised any Jewish traditions, particularly because his old man had never continued with them after Freya's death, nor had he had any wish to learn more about it because it would have reminded him of her.

After Kimberly and her family went back home, all the excitement of the celebrations ended and everything went back to normal, a typically dull period of darkness and cold in the month of January. It was then George started to feel anxious because the sensation of pressure and tightness in his chest reappeared. Mentioning nothing to Sarah, he blamed it on all the excesses of food he'd eaten during the holiday period. He also hadn't heard anything from the production team for a while, another cause of anxiety.

"It must be because of the holiday period," said Sarah while taking down and packing all Christmas decorations.

On the one hand, George was relieved that nothing had been found so far, but on the other hand, he couldn't help being curious about whether they would be able to uncover any relatives of Freya.

Finally, one Tuesday evening near the end of January 2023, after a few months of research, George received a call from the production team when he was travelling home from work.

"Have you found something?" he asked, showing his interest.

"Yes, we have! We're coordinating with the German side and would like to schedule a filming slot when the program presenter comes to deliver the findings to you," the producer explained. "We would rather do it soon as it's rather urgent," he added.

"What have you found? Is there anything you could tell me now if it's something urgent?" asked George, dumbfounded and curious.

"I'm afraid it's part of the procedure for the program presenter to deliver the findings and results to you," the man said patiently but firmly.

"Erm…"

"Would this Saturday be suitable?"

"This Saturday!" exclaimed George.

"Yes. As explained, we would like to do it as soon as possible. I will send you further details in the coming days."

George was frustrated and worried after the call. "Is there something wrong? Why can't they tell me over the phone?" George alerted Sarah to his concerns.

"It's good that they found something. Don't worry, we've watched the program many times and it's part of the selling point of the show for the program presenter to deliver the findings. We already knew your mother died, so there shouldn't be anything too unexpected!"

"But why did they say it's rather urgent?" George wondered, feeling ill at ease.

"I don't know! Try not to worry. The filming is already scheduled to take place this weekend. I'll talk to Kimberly and you should contact Aileen to update her. How are you feeling?"

"I'm fine. I guess. It's like a dream." George let out a deep breath.

The days of waiting seemed like an eternity until finally, the filming day arrived.

George hadn't slept a bit the night before, or rather for several nights. He got up early feeling nauseous. He nevertheless got himself ready and went down to the kitchen to make himself a cup of tea. While waiting for the kettle to boil he felt unsettled with mixed emotions. He looked out the window. *What a cloudy day.* The gloomy weather reflected how he had been feeling ever since he was notified by the producer about the urgency of the filming.

"You're up early. You making tea?" Sarah's voice came from behind him which gave George a fright.

"I wasn't able to sleep anyway so thought I might as well get up. I feel like I'm going to be on a reality show."

"It *is* a reality TV show!" pointed out Sarah. They both guffawed.

"I guess..." said George not sounding very enthusiastic at that moment. He handed a cup of tea to Sarah.

"Try not to overthink it. After all, it's too late to back out. You will find out soon enough about the search."

After breakfast, while George and Sarah were going through all the photos and documents and certificates, George received a call informing him that the program presenter and other crewmembers were about fifteen minutes away.

Stay calm! George told himself while taking a few deep breaths. But that moment of tranquillity was short-lived. Not long after their flat was cramped with people.

George recognised the program presenter straight away after he opened the door but he seemed taller and of bigger build on TV than in person.

Once everyone had been introduced and had greeted each other, Sarah went to the kitchen and was busy making beverages while George focused on the presenter and filming director. They explained to him about the filming procedures of the day while the rest of the team was busy setting up lighting and sound systems and also moving around furniture pieces in the living room.

"The section where I was driving here to meet you has already been recorded. The filming today at first will be bits and pieces. It'll begin with me arriving in your building and ringing your intercom. Once I'm in the building I'll knock on your door and then you welcome me in," explained the presenter while pointing at the main entrance door to the flat.

"OK, should it just be me or Sarah as well welcoming you?"

"It should be both of you. We'll all sit in the living room first for a short introductory talk then Sarah will leave—"

"Wait, Sarah, come here. You need to listen to this," interrupted George.

The presenter explained to Sarah again what he'd already told George.

"And then what happens after?" Sarah looked at the presenter for further instructions.

"I will have a talk with George before I deliver the findings to him. Don't worry, it's not live so we can always cut and re-edit," he assured them.

George and Sarah nodded their heads fiercely.

"Also, we can stop at any time if there's something you don't understand," interjected the filming director.

"Sound checks. Can you count one, two, three, please?" A crewmember attached small microphones to George, Sarah and the presenter. Just as they were watching staff adjusting the lighting, a makeup artist came in as well.

Once the preparations had been completed, they filmed the first segment with the presenter knocking on the door and being welcomed by Sarah and George who led him into the living room as scripted.

"I'll leave you now." After the short introductory talk, Sarah gave George an encouraging hug and patted his shoulder. "Good luck," she whispered in his ear then walked to the kitchen.

"Cut! Great. Ready for the next scene?" the director asked, looking at George and the presenter.

"Err…" George mumbled. Feeling exposed and alone, nerves started to creep up on him as he held a hand to his chest.

Up to that point, George had been feeling at ease because he was preoccupied with so many things happening at the same time that he didn't have the chance to digest everything till Sarah left so the next segment of the filming could start.

"Are we ready?" the presenter asked while he checked with the director with a quick glance.

"Wait, I need a moment! Sarah!" George yelled for his wife with a broken voice. His face turned red as he tried to speak louder but his throat was as dry as sandpaper.

"What is it?" asked Sarah, entering the living room with a swift pace. She saw the sweat on George's forehead. She went to hold his hands and he squeezed back.

"Drink some water." Sarah handed him a glass of water from the table. She held his hand to comfort him while a makeup artist did a retouch.

"OK, are we ready to shoot now?" the presenter gently asked, directing a look at George and Sarah.

"I better leave you now." Sarah squeezed George's hand once more. She turned to go, giving George a final encouraging glance before she left the room.

"Aye. I'm ready," replied George and let out a deep breath.

The presenter and the director exchanged a quick glance with each other and nodded silently.

"Three, two, one…" the director cued with his fingers while counting down. "Action!"

"George, tell us again the reason for your search?" asked the presenter.

"So my birth mother, Freya, was a Jew and was married and had a child in Germany. Both her husband and their son were killed by the Nazis and for some reason she was spared. She was later saved by the liberation army when Germany lost the war. She first went to London then to Edinburgh where she met my father and later they got married," George paused feeling an itching in his throat.

"Do you want some water?"

"Oh, thanks." George took a sip before he continued. "She committed suicide when I was about two, so I never knew her because my father never said anything about her to me when he was alive. When I was about three, he remarried a woman called Aileen, who I always called Mum. She's very supportive of this search. My father died about two years ago so..." George couldn't finish his sentence because he was getting breathless.

"Take your time," calmly said the presenter.

"So I would love to find any relatives of my birth mother so that I can know more about her."

"How come you haven't done it earlier, or have you tried?"

"No, because without the help of this show, I would not even know how and where to begin. After my father died, I found a photo of my birth mother and her first son in Germany and it sparked a kind of curiosity," said George, showing and pointing at the photo of Tomer, the one that Kimberly had found of him on his first birthday.

"What would this search mean for you and your family?" The presenter tilted his head slightly to the side, anticipating an answer from George.

"A closure or new beginnings, I don't know. No words can describe the importance of knowing something, anything at all about my birth mother. I would also like my daughter and her children to know more about her and their Jewish heritage."

"Well, this search has been very special for many reasons. We found something—"

"What? What did you find?" George eagerly burst in.

"With your DNA, we found a connection with a woman called Nadine. She's a granddaughter of your mother's son!"

"What do you mean?" asked George, in a disbelieving tone with his eyes wide open.

"We found your mother's son, your half-brother."

"My mother's son? My mother's son was killed during the war when he was a wee boy!" stated George, perplexed. What he heard sent a chill down his spine and he felt the hair on the back of his neck stand up.

"Apparently not. Tomer, though his name is now Fredrich. He was adopted after the war. He was first living with an old woman who took care of him, but not properly due to her ill health. From our research and the official adoption file of Fredrich, we found that he was rescued from this old lady's home and that the old woman's daughter had worked as a guard in a concentration camp. After the war, this guard was put on trial for war crimes and somehow it was discovered she had hidden this boy in her mother's home. She refused to reveal where or from who she got this boy. She later committed suicide in prison before the trial was over."

"But, but, my birth mother committed suicide because she felt so guilty that her first husband and their son were killed and not her! She couldn't live with herself even though she got remarried and had another child. I can't believe he's still alive!"

"George, do you want to speak to your half-brother Tomer, now called Fredrich?" asked the presenter.

"What do you mean? How?" shouted George in total amazement with his eyes wide open. No one could even come close to grasping the degree of George's internal turmoil and shock at that moment.

"We have organised a video call. Normally, we would arrange for you to fly over there or for him to come here but unfortunately he's in bad health and we want to make sure there is still time."

"My goodness! There is so much to take in... Of course, I want to talk to my half-brother," announced George without any hesitation, almost as if he was afraid the opportunity would be taken away from him.

A crewmember quickly set up a screen and it was connected to a live feed from Germany. It was being filmed in a hospice where George first saw in the background a man in his mid-eighties attached to an endotracheal tube. The screen then turned to a young lady who was introduced by the presenter as the granddaughter of Fredrich, formerly named Tomer.

"Hi," greeted the young lady.

"Hello!" George managed to force the word out of his mouth but was otherwise totally stunned.

"My name is Nadine. I'm the granddaughter of Fredrich. Nice to meet you!" she said in good English.

Nadine then explained to George that Fredrich's adopted family had been open with him about his circumstances, and growing up he was always curious about his birth parents. He didn't do any research as an adult because he didn't want to upset his adoptive parents. Life went on, he got married and had children and then grandchildren. Nadine was very close to Fredrich and knew the deepest wish to search for his past had always been at the back of his mind. The previous year Fredrich had become quite ill, so Nadine submitted her DNA test and initiated the search knowing Fredrich didn't have long to live.

"I didn't tell my granddad or anyone in my family at first because I didn't want them to be disappointed if nothing was found. My granddad is delighted that my DNA led to finding you."

"What an amazing story!" George told her. "Err, it sounds like you have a hint of a Scottish accent?" he added.

"As it happens, I did my master's degree in Glasgow!"

Again, George was speechless at how fate had brought them together and he realised that their paths could have even crossed before when Nadine lived in Glasgow and they never would have known it.

"My granddad would like to say hello." Nadine removed herself from the main screen and brought the camera closer to Fredrich. She pulled down the ventilation mask from Fredrich's face.

"Hello," whispered Fredrich, with great effort. He looked frail but somehow managed to raise his hand holding a copy of a photo of him when he was a little baby. He pointed at the photo and then pointed back at himself. It was the same photo that George had submitted for the search; the exact photo George was holding in his hand of Tomer.

"Hello." Unconsciously, tears flowed down George's face. He too pointed at the photo and then at Fredrich. His heart was filled with mixed emotions of sorrow, happiness and surprise.

The main screen switched back to Nadine. "It was thanks to the photo you submitted that we learned the real age and birthday of my granddad." Nadine took the photo from Fredrich and turned to the back showing the faded writing Tomer geboren 18. Juli 1939. "Also, we're forever grateful to have photos of Freya!"

George sobbed and uttered a sudden loud cry that prompted Sarah to pop her head through the doorway to see what was happening.

The filming ended with the presenter telling them that they had organised for George and Sarah to fly to Germany a few days later to meet Fredrich and the filming team and the presenter would also follow along.

Less than two hours later, everyone from the TV program had finally gone and George and Sarah were left alone. They felt a sudden void as everything became so quiet in the mid-afternoon light. George and Sarah looked at each other without uttering a word, both trying their best to digest and absorb all that they had been told.

"I need to lie down," said George, touching his chest with his right hand, seemingly showing signs of exhaustion.

"Is anything the matter?" asked Sarah, alarmed.

"I just need to rest a bit. Wake me up in an hour or so. I don't want to sleep too long or I won't sleep this evening," he replied while he felt a spasm in his hand muscle and his chest area tightened up.

"Here, drink some water." Sarah handed George a glass of water and watched as he went to the bedroom.

Sarah sat quietly for a few minutes before she called Kimberly and updated her about today's filming process and the extraordinary findings about Fredrich, her dad's half-brother. They chatted away and suddenly Sarah heard a sound coming from the bedroom of an object dropping on the floor. She rushed to the bedroom and first saw the glass of water splashed all over the floor and saw George slumped in pain.

"What's going on?" cried Sarah in confusion.

"Call an ambulance," muttered George, his tone letting her know he was in real trouble.

"Where is it hurting?" asked Sarah, with a growing sense of dread.

George pointed at the left side of his chest, unable to speak. He was covered in cold sweat and frowning. George always teased Sarah about making a storm in a teacup concerning his health so for him to ask for an ambulance she knew it was serious. She rushed back to the kitchen in panic for the phone and heard Kimberly on the other end.

"Mum, are you there? What's happening?" Kimberley was anxious at the sudden interruption.

"Kim, your father needs an ambulance!" She hung up as Kimberly was asking what was wrong with her father. While walking back to the bedroom she quickly dialled 999.

Sarah looked at George in bed, his eyes closed and his features twisted with pain. She was petrified about what was happening but had to hold herself together and not burst into tears while talking to the operator and doing her best to report the details to the emergency response service.

"Stay calm, love. Everything will be all right." Sarah adjusted the duvet so that George was fully covered and told him that the ambulance was on its way.

George opened his eyes as a small sign of acknowledgement.

"What can I do to make you better? Do you want some water?" Sarah asked, an attempt to occupy herself in order not to lose it.

"No," George responded in a weak voice while forcing a smile on his face. "No thank you, I meant to say…"

"Oh, you silly sod. Don't make jokes now," pleaded Sarah, her voice cracked and tears forming in her eyes. "I will be right back."

Sarah ran back and forward a few times from the bedroom to the living room and looked out the window at the street in front of the building. About twenty minutes after placing the call she heard the sound of sirens nearing.

"It must be the ambulance I called! I'll go and meet them." Sarah gave George a light squeeze to his hand.

She ran to the front of her apartment and opened the door. Sure enough, she saw the ambulance in front of her building and two ambulance staff taking down a wheeled stretcher. Sarah shouted and waved at them to make them aware of which floor she was on. She saw a few curious neighbours popping out of their homes and standing either on their balconies or in the communal courtyard area to see what was happening.

She pressed the buzzer of the intercom as soon as she heard it and ran to the elevator to wait for the emergency team.

"Are you the one who called?" one of them directed the question at Sarah as he caught sight of her waiting outside the lift.

"Yes, I'm his wife. Thanks for coming so quickly! This way." Sarah led them to their home.

"Can you tell me where you're hurting?" asked one of the paramedics as soon as he entered the bedroom while the other one took notes.

George pointed at his chest area and his left arm.

"Have you been throwing up or had a fever?"

George shook his head.

After a few further questions, the paramedics transferred George to a wheeled stretcher.

"OK, we're now going to take him to the emergency room. You're allowed to come with us."

Sarah closed the door behind her and then ran past the wheeled stretcher and pressed the lift button. She waved distractedly to a few familiar faces when saw some neighbours gathered around the ambulance parked in the front of the building.

Once the crew had loaded George and Sarah into the vehicle, they roared off.

"We're measuring your blood pressure, heartbeat and doing a few other tests," explained one of the paramedics to George as Sarah listened. At the same time, the man was making notes. He then contacted the hospital to inform them of their imminent arrival.

With the intense medical lighting, she saw stripes of makeup from the earlier filming running down across George's face. A sudden unpleasant thought jumped into Sarah's mind. It wasn't her first time riding in an ambulance. She'd accompanied her mother in an ambulance to the hospital about ten years earlier. Her mother never came home; she'd died in the hospital. Sarah shook her head to focus on George. Sarah reached out to hold George's hand. At that moment she somehow found the strength to remain calm because she knew she had to be strong for both of them.

Today he just learned that his half-brother was alive so he must *pull through,* she thought. "I love you. I'm here for you. We'll be in this together," Sarah leaned over and whispered in George's ear to ease the fear she saw in his eyes.

Once they'd arrived at the hospital, George was taken straight away to the emergency room.

Sarah stayed in the waiting room where she found a moment to call Kimberly. "The doctors are doing some tests on your father. Don't worry, darling, he will pull through this," assured Sarah. She could only hear Kimberly sobbing on the other end.

After the call with Kimberly, Sarah anxiously waited in the waiting room. *Did I shut and lock the door properly? Did I leave the oven on?* As they'd left in a hurry and in such unsettling circumstances her head had started to spin.

To be on the safe side and to calm her mind, she sent a text to a neighbour to check. She then fiddled with her phone and absently turned it off and on a few times. She thought of getting a cup of coffee but didn't want to leave, afraid of missing something if doctors or nurses wanted to talk to her. Her eyes were glued to the door of the emergency room. The question *What if* kept repeating in her head.

After about half an hour of waiting the doctor came out and invited Sarah into a small consultation room nearby.

"Your husband suffered from myocardial infarction," said the doctor as he pointed to a monitor screen showing a black and white scan taken of George's heart. The doctor showed her the offending blockages.

Sarah looked at the doctor in total shock without knowing what to say. She'd never heard the term myocardial infarction before nor did she fully grasp what the doctor had shown her.

"It was lucky you contacted the emergency services so quickly because it's rather life-threatening if not treated immediately. There are a few possible treatments but the best option is surgery to perform a bypass in order to create new routes through which blood can flow around any blocked or narrowed arteries," the doctor explained.

He also informed Sarah about the other treatments and the pros and cons of each. He then went on to give more details about the suggested operation and possible complications that might occur after the procedure. For Sarah it was all too much, she was not in a mental or emotional state to absorb all that information. She just nodded on seeing the doctor's mouth moving and signed a consent form and a few more documents to agree to the recommended surgery.

"We will schedule this surgery procedure as soon as possible today. You—"

"I will wait here," quickly announced Sarah. She was afraid the doctor might suggest otherwise. "Oh sorry, I jumped in before you finished!"

The doctor grinned and showed no sign of being offended. He continued, "OK, you can wait in the waiting room and we will inform you about the outcome right after, but you won't be able to see him until tomorrow I'm afraid. He will be monitored in the intensive care unit overnight after the surgery."

Sarah once again sat in the waiting room. In that moment she felt so hopeless and sorry for herself, and she sobbed quietly in a corner not wanting to draw attention. She wiped her tears with her sleeve and exhaled slowly. Her shoulders dropped for a short moment as her tension eased but then a thousand worried thoughts appeared in her mind. *I need to call Kimberly. She must be worried sick*. At that moment she realised her phone was switched off. As soon as she turned it on she saw a text message from her neighbour informing her that the door was properly locked and asked if everything was OK with George. She sent a quick reply of thanks. Sarah also noticed there were many missed calls from Kimberly. She was about to press Kimberly's number when the phone rang. She jumped in surprise and her posture tensed.

"Mum, how is Dad? What did the doctor say?" came Kimberley's anxious voice.

In one breath Sarah updated Kimberly about the situation and managed to persuade her there was no need for her to rush to Edinburgh immediately. "I will call you once I know more."

"Don't switch off your phone again!" ordered her daughter.

After Sarah hung up, her mind went blank. As if watching a silent movie in slow motion she saw hospital staff, patients, and family members moving in and out of the emergency unit. For a few moments, she held both hands over her face in fear and exhaustion. *What if.* The question appeared again. To distract herself from her thoughts she looked around and heard sirens, cries, footsteps rushing, phone calls and the sound of the emergency room doors opening and closing.

I'm so tired. Sarah was truly worn out and as soon as she closed her eyes she fell asleep for a good while. She was then woken up by the ringing of her phone. It took her a few moments to register where she was. She quickly answered and it was Kimberly again.

"Mum, how are you holding up?" Kimberly asked, worried.

"I'm OK. I'm just exhausted," she replied, her energy levels as low as her mood. She adjusted her posture that had been stiffly frozen for the past two hours or so. She looked up and saw a clock displaying the time and realised it was more than four hours since they'd arrived here, Sarah counting in her head.

"Nana, Nana."

Sarah heard her grandchildren calling in the background and Kimberly calming them, "Mummy is busy with Grandma now. We'll call tomorrow and you can talk to her then. Cam, can you take them to the living room? I need to talk to my mum!" Kimberly called out.

Hearing her grandchildren's voices boosted her energy and at the same time, Sarah became emotional again.

"Mum, I'm back. I Googled myocardial infarction and found out a bit about follow-up treatments and changes in lifestyle after the operation. I think one thing Dad needs to do is to lose weight. You'll need to control his intake of food and soft drinks. He won't lose weight if he keeps drinking Coke and stuff like that. It'd be best if he cut out any kind of fizzy drinks, including sugar-free ones. Don't you agree?"

Sarah refrained herself from bursting into laughter imagining how impossible it would be to prohibit George from drinking his beloved carbonated drinks. "Wait, someone is coming to talk to me. I will call you back."

"The operation went well and now he's resting," said the man, a male nurse who had come to update her. "He will be monitored in the intensive care unit for the night, and if everything goes well he will be transferred to a regular hospital room tomorrow. You should really go home get some rest and come back tomorrow during visiting hours. Don't worry, we'll call you to inform you which ward he's in!" the nurse said with a big smile to ease Sarah's concerns.

"Thank you! I'll... er... I'll be back tomorrow." Sarah barely recognised the sound of her own voice. She was thirsty and had difficulty articulating her words.

As she dragged her feet out of the emergency unit, she felt as though every bone in her body was aching. She had trouble putting one foot in front of the other because she had been holding tension in her neck and body and was stiff all over. She hesitated for a moment on the pavement outside but decided to take a taxi home. She could count on her fingers the number of times she'd taken taxis, but she was mentally and physically too tired to deal with the bus. She just wanted to get home.

Chapter 12 – 2023

Sarah got home and straight away walked to her bedroom. She plunged onto the bed, fully clothed and still with her shoes on. Just before she fell asleep she suddenly sat up and remembered she needed to call Kimberly. She took a few moments to collect her thoughts and then reached for her phone. She saw more missed calls from her daughter. She had deliberately switched her phone to silent mode earlier so she changed the mode back. Her head was pounding and her throat was hurting.

Sarah walked in the dark to the bathroom. She brushed her teeth and with foam in her mouth, she looked up. She spat it out and in the small dim light above the mirror on the front of the medicine cabinet she saw an older version of herself staring back at her. She could not recall the last time she'd closely looked at herself. Maybe it was the lighting but she hardly recognised this face of sunken eyes and messy hair. She pulled up the excess skin on her neck and as she let it go it sagged droopily having lost its elasticity. She felt as though she'd become this old overnight. *My goodness, how come I haven't noticed so many wrinkles and dark spots on my face before?* Sarah then opened the medicine cabinet and reached for a pack of ibuprofen. She swallowed two tablets along with a large glass of water in one go. Cough! She choked and spat water into the sink and felt her shoulders relax. Just as she walked back to her bed the phone rang again and she grabbed it to answer immediately.

"Mum, are you OK? How is Dad? Where are you now?" Kimberly burst out with questions as soon as Sarah answered.

"Sorry, love. Listen, I meant to call you but I just got home. The operation went well and I should be able to see him tomorrow. I'm knackered and I need to lie down," Sarah declared, feeling totally drained.

"Thank God! I'm worried about you though. It's Sunday tomorrow so I'll come down with Cameron and the kids. Cameron can drive back with the kids tomorrow afternoon after they've visited Dad in the hospital but I'll take a few days off and stay with you."

"You don't need to come down."

"It would provide an opportunity to catch up with admin paperwork and reports that I could do remotely. Besides, being away from Cameron and the kids for a few days would be like a mini vacation for me," joked Kimberly. The truth was that without a shadow of a doubt, she recognised how much Sarah needed support. Knowing her father, he'd not be easy to care for.

Sarah laughed and stretched her upper body. She felt her head still hurting and hoped those painkillers she'd taken would kick in soon.

"OK. Let's discuss it more tomorrow. My brain can't take in more information right now!" Sarah tried to make light of the situation.

"Get some sleep now. Talk to you tomorrow."

After she disconnected the call, Sarah turned the phone on silent mode again and then decided to turn it off altogether. She took off her shoes and undressed, lifted the duvet and climbed inside, all in robotic fashion. Her head was still working through all the events and emotions of the day. Her stomach made a growling sound that was a signal that with everything that'd happened that day, she hadn't eaten anything properly since breakfast. Not that she had any appetite, yet still she was debating with herself whether it was worth getting up to eat something. Suddenly she grasped it wasn't a good idea to turn off the phone in case the hospital wanted to reach her. She turned on the phone again and found relaxing sleep music on YouTube that helped her to drift off, eventually.

She slept about ten hours straight and the next morning woke up just after eight and felt fresh, but her perky mood was short-lived. She went to the kitchen craving a cup of coffee and saw piles of cups and plates left on the sink from yesterday's filming and that brought back her feelings of anxiety, especially thinking about George in the hospital. Sarah put the dishes in the dishwasher and put on the kettle.

After she'd enjoyed her much-needed cup of coffee, Sarah sat in the kitchen and took a deep breath before she pressed Kimberly's number on speed dial.

"Good morning! Are you still coming?" Sarah asked, stretching her arm.

"Good morning to you too. We're already on the road. The kids are still sleeping in the back seat. We should reach your place just after ten. Have you heard from the hospital?" asked Kimberly with a hint of worry in her tone.

"Wow, you're early. No, nothing yet. They promised to call before noon. Hey, drive carefully!"

"We will. Cameron and I'll take turns to drive. See you soon."

Just before Kimberly arrived Sarah received a phone call from the hospital informing her that George had been released from the intensive care unit and transferred to a regular ward and that she would be able to visit him from two p.m.

When two o'clock came, Sarah and Kimberly's family arrived at the hospital right on time after having their lunch at a nearby McDonald's.

George's eyes lit up as soon as they met with Sarah's.

"Love, how are you?" Sarah held his hand and leaned over and kissed George's forehead.

George wasn't able to speak. Holding back tears George weakly nodded his head, looking frail and sorrowful.

Sarah held back her emotions because she didn't want to make him more upset.

"Guess what, Kim and Cameron are here with the kids. They're waiting outside. Should I get them? We were not sure if you'd be ready to see so many people at once."

George's answering smile showed his delight.

"Granddad, Granddad." Kimberly's kids ran into the room with excitement as soon as they heard Sarah calling them. They jumped up and down eagerly showing George a get-well card they'd made for him the night before and photos of their dog that they'd recently adopted from an animal shelter.

"Hey, easy there! Your granddad just had surgery," warned Kimberly.

George's mood picked up with his family around him. They all laughed when he pulled a face describing the bland and tasteless food the hospital served.

"Go and get Granddad a can of Coke," said George half-jokingly with a wink to Kimberly's children.

"You can't be serious, Dad! Joke as you want. We have to take control of your sugar intake now, and your diet," announced Kimberly. She was not amused by George's banter and gave her dad a stern look to show she meant it.

"Let's talk about it later." Sarah quickly jumped in so that George would not feel attacked and overwhelmed, even though she was in total agreement with Kimberly that this was a subject that they had to tackle sooner rather than later.

"What will happen with your trip to Germany?" Right after she raised the question, Kimberly held up her hand signalling Sarah to wait before answering. She gestured at her husband. "Cam, can you take the kids to the cafeteria or TV room? They're driving me mad fighting over whose turn it's to play with the tablet."

Cameron duly shepherded the children in the direction of the hospital cafeteria. Kimberly turned her attention back to her parents and waited for Sarah to answer her question.

"When the hospital phoned this morning the doctor strongly suggested that your father is not to fly for some time after the surgery," she explained. With a glance at George, she saw how doleful he was.

"OK, I will call the TV production people tomorrow and let them know the circumstances. By the way, should we inform Nan about your surgery?"

Simultaneously, both George and Sarah shook their heads because they didn't want to worry Aileen, especially as she was so far away. In any case, the surgery had already happened and it had gone well so there was no reason to cause her stress at that point.

Sarah and Kimberly's family left the hospital after the visiting hour was over. Cameron dropped Sarah and Kimberly off at Sarah's and he drove back to Aberdeen with the kids as they had school the following day.

The next day while Sarah went to work, Kimberly informed George's workplace about his operation. She also called the TV production team and asked that Nadine and her family in Germany be informed about the situation too. They then had a long chat, discussing how to go further with the filming but without any concrete decision being reached because everything depended on George's recovery.

Sarah and Kimberly came to see George every day. Sure enough, as Kimberly had predicted, George was more than a handful. Instead of being grateful that he'd survived the ordeal and surgery, he was sullen, bickering with them about trivial matters. They understood he was merely acting out about his frustration and disappointment not to be able to fly to Germany to meet his half-brother. Many times they had to bite their tongues but their limits were certainly tested.

"What a load of crap!" complained George, glowering as he raised his hand holding a leaflet the doctor had left him about rehabilitation and aftercare that included exercise, stress management techniques, counselling and lifestyle changes. That included a healthy diet to reduce the chances of future heart disease.

"Stop being a child. The doctors have your best interest at heart." Sarah also raised her voice at George occasionally when he started to sound like a broken record, constantly complaining about the same things and refusing to comply with the doctor's advice about aftercare once he got out of the hospital.

"Dad, you have to be reasonable! You simply must change your lifestyle, exercise more and eat healthier!" Kimberly joined in to support her mother.

"You're giving me a headache, both of you!" George turned his head away and sulked in silence as a sign of protest.

Sarah and Kimberly gave each other a quick knowing look, a sign of agreement that it would be a long battle and they would have to work with George bit by bit.

Despite his moaning and complaining to Sarah and Kimberly, over the time he spent in the hospital he got on well with the nurses and doctors. More than once he urged Sarah to bring cakes on the day of his release for the unit as a token to thank the doctors and staff for taking good care of him.

The day before George's release from his five-night stay in the hospital, Kimberly was in the kitchen checking her emails waiting for her mother to get back from her work.

"I could murder a cup of tea," shouted Sarah to her from the entry hallway, kicking off her shoes and hanging up her jacket.

"Good afternoon. Nice to see you too," teased Kimberly. "Bad day, huh? Come and sit down. I will make you a cuppa. Oh, I also baked a pie." Kimberly put the kettle on and cut the pie in slices.

"Oh, silly people at work. I… Wait, let's talk about something else. How was your day?" Sarah came to the kitchen and slumped into the chair. She massaged her neck firmly hoping to release the tightness.

Kimberly handed Sarah her cup and a piece of pie. "I went to Nan's place and sorted out her post and watered her plants," reported Kimberly about her day to Sarah. "Oh, I'm constantly checking updates online about my train back to Aberdeen. Apparently, there are disruptions because of either strikes or repair work."

"Yes, I heard that too. When is the next bus? You know how sulky your dad can be if we come late," Sarah joked while pulling a face.

"Mum, let's spoil ourselves for once. I already ordered an Uber for us. It's really not that expensive."

Sarah and Kimberly stayed on a bit longer enjoying their time together, a once-in-a-blue-moon occasion with just the two of them. They enthusiastically discussed trying out new hairstyles at their hairdresser's appointment the next morning before Kimberly's train back home.

"How is Cameron doing with the kids?"

"To me, they didn't say anything but Cameron told me they missed me reading their bedtime stories."

They were in the midst of laughing and talking about how Cameron was dealing with the kids in Kimberly's absence when Sarah's phone rang which startled them both.

"Hope it's not from the hospital?" Sarah voiced her worry. She answered it immediately without checking the number and felt a sickening feeling in her stomach.

"Yes, I understand. Can you hold on for a sec?" Sarah covered the phone with her hand and repeated to Kimberly what she'd just heard from the TV production member. "Apparently, Nadine is asking to speak to your dad and it's rather urgent. She's asked to be connected on video call."

Kimberly took a quick glance at her watch and then stretched out her hand asking for the phone.

"Hi, this is Kimberly, daughter of George. We're on our way to the hospital. Our Uber is literally on its way. I'll bring my laptop. Please send me or my mum the link to the call and I'll set it up once I get there."

Kimberly had previously asked the TV team for Nadine's contact details to inform her about George's situation but was told that all communications must be arranged through the production crew. In the contract George had signed they were not to have direct contact with each other until they met face to face, in the presence of the TV crew. However, it was made clear to Sarah and Kimberly that the video call that day would not be filmed nor would any TV crew be present.

How peculiar. What could it be? Why would Nadine want to speak to George urgently? Hope Fredrich is OK! With those alarming questions and worrying thoughts in their minds, they were on their way to the hospital.

Once they reached George's room, Kimberly explained the request from Nadine to him and also warned the other patient sharing the room, who'd just moved in two nights ago. Kimberly drew the partition curtain so their section was secluded. They held their breath in suspense and one could cut the tension with a knife while they were waiting for Kimberly to set up the video call. George and Sarah looked at each other, both thinking the worst but not able to admit it to each other or to themselves.

"Should I change?" breaking the silence, George asked Sarah as he pointed at his pyjamas.

"No need. No time!" Sarah shook her head, short with her answer. She approached his bed adjusted his pillow so he was sitting up straight and used her fingers to arrange his hair.

"Dad, you're now connected." Kimberly gave George a signal and moved away from the screen.

"Can you hear me?" Nadine asked, appearing on the screen.

"Yes, we can hear you," answered George, Sarah and Kimberly at once and waved simultaneously.

"Good. I can hear you too. Hi George," greeted Nadine with a wave back.

From the screen, George saw quite a number of people next to Nadine. Apart from her, George only vaguely recognised her parents.

"Sorry to bring you bad news when you just had surgery. Hope your recovery went well. My granddad is deteriorating and the doctor said it's near. We just want to call so that you've got a chance to say goodbye."

"What do you mean to say goodbye?" George's mind went blank. He refused to register what was presented in front of him.

"Here is my granddad. The doctor said he will not last much longer." Nadine adjusted her computer screen, showing Fredrich lying in the bed hooked up to a mechanical ventilator, looking distant and not responsive.

"How could it be! I don't understand. I just got to know about your existence last week!" George choked up.

Sarah and Kimberly were next to him and the room was filled with the downhearted atmosphere.

"Dad, can you see, Nadine put a picture of us on the pillow next to Fredrich's head." With her voice cracking, Kimberly directed George's attention to the photo that George had submitted for the TV search.

George was in total denial and not able to acknowledge anything that was being said.

"Opa," softly called Nadine in Fredrich's ear and rubbed her hand gently on his shoulder. She pulled the ventilator mask away from his mouth. "Kannst du mich hören? Kannst du George von mir grüßen?"

At first, Fredrich didn't respond but then his eyes opened slightly wider when he heard the sound of George's name but was too weak to speak.

Nadine put the mask right back when she noticed Fredrich started breathing heavily with difficulty. She turned and talked to the screen. "I'm sorry, he's no longer conscious. I'm so sorry you won't have the chance to meet him in person. I—"

"Nadine. Nadine. Schau!" Nadine was interrupted by loud shouts from her family.

Nadine looked over her shoulder and saw a frail but noticeable movement of Fredrich's hand. She quickly moved away from the screen and alerted George that he should watch as there was a visible movement up and down of Frederich's hand. Once… twice… and then the moment halted.

No one knew whether Fredrich was conscious and still there at that moment or whether his journey had already started and he was away, somewhere, free from the prison that his body had become. Nevertheless, at that moment from both sides of the family, they all wanted to believe that it was his last message in this world, his farewell to a brother who he had never got to know or meet in person.

"Goodbye Fredrich. Bye-bye Fredrich," George, Kimberly and Sarah tearfully repeated, waving their hands, not able to take their eyes away from the sight of Fredrich through the computer screen.

Fredrich died two hours later.

For years to come, the thought of Fredrich's gesture as saying his farewell gave George a sense of peace of mind. It was a closure that was much needed for him to find solace for the years apart, the injustice, the losses they had suffered. It helped to soothe the hurt and the painful memories of all that had happened in their lives.

Chapter 13 – 2023

George was ordered by the doctor to be monitored in the hospital for two more days, longer than originally scheduled as he'd experienced abnormality of the heart's rhythm after receiving the news about the death of Fredrich. At first, he was clearly upset and saddened but then became very quiet and emotionally withdrawn. Kimberly had to go back to Aberdeen and it left Sarah with the heavy burden of picking up the pieces.

On the day of George's discharge from the hospital, Sarah came to bring him home. She had taken a few days off work so she could keep a closer eye on him.

After George got the all-clear sign and was discharged by the doctor, Sarah packed all his belongings in a bag and double-checked they hadn't forgotten anything while George sat in an armchair beside the window looking out. She took a quick glance at him and couldn't help feeling deflated when she saw his numb demeanour and emptiness in his expression.

"Do you want to take these home?" Sarah pointed at the flowers sent by his colleagues and some neighbours.

"Naw," said George as he turned the corners of his mouth up in a sign of indifference. He stood up and walked towards the door in such haste, indicating he couldn't get out of there soon enough. "Ready?"

Standing behind him Sarah noticed George seemingly limping and dragging his feet more than usual. Sarah believed it was an issue caused by bad blood circulation. Being in the hospital lying in bed without much exercise had taken a toll on him. It was on the tip of her tongue to mention it to him but thought at the last moment not to put further pressure on him. Instead, she just followed him out after their goodbyes to the hospital staff.

"Oh, great. It's wet," George complained when they exited the hospital.

"Yes. Phew," Sarah sighed, waiting for George to make a suggestion about getting home.

"It's only drizzling," he said and pointed in the direction of the bus stop not far away. It didn't occur to him to offer to take a taxi because it simply wasn't something he was familiar with.

Sarah nodded, hiding her irritation. She bit her lip not saying a word because she was not in the mood to start an argument. She felt vulnerable and somewhat disappointed in herself for not speaking her mind.

On the bus ride and subsequent walk home, they hardly spoke to each other; they were preoccupied with their own thoughts. Once they got home, George excused himself and headed straight to the bedroom for a wee lie down.

"You can't go to bed wet," pointed out Sarah, tossing him a towel she got from their bathroom.

Sarah then dried her own hair and went to the kitchen, unpacking their things and turning on the washing machine. A few stray raindrops from her hair trickled down her back; she felt the chill. A sudden sense of tiredness overcame her. She sat down for a while without being able to focus on anything in her mind. She massaged her legs trying to ease the stiffness. She was contemplating how to break it to Aileen about George's operation and most worryingly about his physical health as well as his mental state. She was also overwhelmingly frustrated with her brother who had dragged out the court case about their father's estate for so long without the slightest progress. Suddenly she started crying, a kind of emotional meltdown. Her tears were a reflection of the intense pressure from everything trapped inside her. She wept uncontrollably and was not bothered that the sound of her heart-rending sobs overpowered the noise of the washing machine. For once in her life she didn't care to hide her despair.

"Sarah, love, are you all right?" asked George worriedly as he turned on the light, appearing in the kitchen to sit next to her.

Rubbing her puffy eyes Sarah had no desire to speak.

George held her hand and sat quietly next to her. "Tell me what's troubling you."

Sarah turned her head, looking him in the eyes, and uttered aloud, "What are we going to do? I don't know how much more I can take!"

"I'm so sorry, love. I've put you through a lot lately," apologised George. He had seldom seen her in such a distressed state.

After a while, she calmed down and grabbed a tissue to wipe off her tears and blow her nose. "I'm better now. I just needed a good cry." She let out a deep breath.

"Thank you for taking care of me in the hospital. I'd not have been alive here today if it weren't for you calling an ambulance," George said sombrely.

"You silly man! Of course, I had to make the call when you were unwell." Sarah stroked George's face with the back of her hand.

"I'll be better!" affirmed George, looking at Sarah with a sincere smile.

"George, we'll take one day at a time but you've got to really make the effort to take care of yourself, right?" she articulated each word for him to understand the seriousness of them.

"Aye. Aye. I promise," George nodded.

"Don't make promises you can't keep!" she told him sternly. Sarah was doubtful if George could stick to his promise because he probably wouldn't be able to come to terms with the real problems facing them, especially concerning his own health and mental state.

"Well. Believe it or not, I weighed myself when we got home and noticed that I had lost half a stone already. The bland food they served in the hospital did the trick and was obviously good for something!" remarked George with a sheepish grin. He laughed weakly in an attempt to cheer her up.

Sarah offered a smile although she felt like a black cloud was still lingering above them. "My goodness, it's a start I suppose. Sit in the living room and watch a bit of

TV. I'll call you when tea is ready. Let's call Aileen later. Isn't she coming back soon?"

"Yes, I noted down the date somewhere when I last talked to her before my surgery but I truly don't remember where I put it," he replied vaguely.

They had their evening meal and much to his surprise, George rather enjoyed it and praised the new healthy cooking recipe Sarah had followed; or at least even he knew that showing anything other than enthusiasm would not have been well received. They were in a better mood by then, agreeing that Sarah should do most of the talking to inform Aileen about the surgery now it was over. She would also know best how to break the news about Fredrich's death, knowing Aileen would be upset for George's sake.

"Hello, how are you?" George and Sarah were sitting straight on their chairs in front of their tablet like two diligent school students as they greeted and waved to Aileen as soon as she was connected.

"Well I'm better now," came the reply as Aileen stood up, holding onto the table and, with the help of crutches, hopped back a few steps to show the plaster on her leg. "I fell and had a minor bone fracture about a week ago on the same leg I twisted last year. The orthopaedic surgeon—"

"Be careful!" both Sarah and George yelled out, holding up their arms in the air as if they could assist Aileen to sit down through the other side of the screen.

"Mum, sit down, slowly! Don't fall. How are you feeling? What did the doctors say?" It was George who came out with the questions.

"My leg is swollen and quite sore. I've to wear the plaster cast for at least three to four weeks to allow the bones to heal. I've been told not to fly before the end of March, I'm afraid."

"But what about Mother's Day this year?" muttered George under his breath, apparently nursing a grievance about Aileen's extended stay in America.

Sarah was astonished at what she heard. She kicked George's leg under the table and simultaneously by reflex she started coughing.

"Are you all right, dear?" asked Aileen in concern.

"Don't worry!" said George and quickly went to fetch Sarah a glass of water.

"Thanks. I'm OK. Just a dry cough." Sarah took a few sips while George stroked her back. What Aileen didn't see was Sarah giving George a quick but firm stare hoping he would get the hint to think before he spoke.

Luckily it seemed that Aileen hadn't heard George's earlier comment.

"Aileen, hope you recover soon. No doubt Alistair and Michelle are taking good care of you," Sarah continued with their conversation.

"Oh, they're taking good care of me just fine. Their kids and grandkids visit often as well. How are things with you two?"

"We have something to tell you."

"What? Don't scare me. Kimberly and her family are well?" Aileen asked in sudden concern.

"Kim and her family are all fine. It's about George."

Sarah then told Aileen about the heart problem and subsequent surgery and that George would need to take sick leave for two months to begin with.

"George just got discharged from the hospital today. I will make sure he follows through with the recovery and rehabilitation programme! When you're back, you can also keep an eye on him," she added and they all had a giggle.

"Oh dear, son! I really hope you recover soon. I'm so sorry that I'm not there with you. Can't believe it happened while I'm away," Aileen told him in obvious worry at the news. "You must take better care of yourself you know!"

"Aileen, there is another thing we need to tell you. It's about the search," Sarah interjected.

"Oh, I meant to call and ask about it but because of my accident, everything was frantic for a few days. What did they find?"

George and Sarah then took turns telling her about Nadine and Tomer and his new adopted name Fredrich and then the call a few days ago when they said goodbye to him.

"My goodness, I don't know what to say! It really breaks my heart hearing this," said Aileen with tears forming in her eyes.

"Yes, we're trying to take it all in as well. Nadine informed us through the TV crew that due to the Jewish tradition, the actual funeral occurred very quickly after the death," Sarah explained.

"What a development! And I would never have thought Freya's son was alive after all those years. How sad it was you never had a chance to really meet him." Aileen held her hands across her mouth in sorrow.

"Yes, it was hard for George to process and accept, but he was very thankful that he was able to say his farewell."

For the rest of the conversation, George sat there arms crossed not talking much apart from nodding and confirming what Sarah was saying. He remained quiet after their call with Aileen. Knowing her husband well, Sarah recognised that his silence spoke volumes about his discontent about something, especially from the perturbed expression on his face.

"What now? Something is troubling you?"

"Maybe... Maybe I should have died of the heart attack so that you all could get on with your lives. I am such a burden to you all," said George with his head down looking at the floor and avoiding eye contact with Sarah.

"Why would you say such a thing?" Raising her eyebrows, Sarah was surprised and not amused by what she just heard.

Still with his head down George was silent again.

"You can't just throw a fit like this and then say nothing," stated Sarah in a challenging tone, waving her hands in the air in annoyance.

"I'm sorry to put you through so much. I would be at a total loss without you. I am sorry. I am sorry," repeated George, feeling ashamed of his earlier outburst.

"I understand that you're dealing with a lot right now but you can't just forget all the other good things in your life. Think how many people love you and how lucky you are to survive the heart surgery," consoled Sarah now holding George's hand.

"I know. I know—"

"You are a great father to Kimberly, not to mention what you mean to her children. You're also a loyal husband and a loving son to Aileen," Sarah pointed out. "Wait, what were you on about Mother's Day when we spoke to Aileen earlier?" asked Sarah not fully understanding why on earth it bothered him so much that she wouldn't be there this year.

"I…"

"What is it?" Sarah insisted.

"Promise you won't be cross with me?"

"That I can't do, but I can promise to listen without interrupting."

"You see, ever since I can remember I have always celebrated Mother's Day with Aileen. This year, finding out about my half-brother and then losing him without being able to meet him before his death really affected me and I thought it would be special for me that she would be here," George confessed.

Sarah nodded in silence as she'd promised, chewing over George's words.

"I know it seems petty but I can't help imagining them being a happy family together celebrating Mother's Day."

"Oh, I didn't think of that. I see why you're upset. But you can't dwell on that or be mad at Aileen for not being able to be here because she's broken her leg! Besides, using your logic, you guys have celebrated Mother's Day together almost all of your life so what's wrong that she's celebrating it this year with Alistair?" Sarah remarked in a soft tone, taking into account his feeling of being excluded.

"I couldn't help thinking that she doesn't want to come back because she'd rather spend her time with Alistair... her real son."

"Oh, George c'mon, don't be daft! You know that isn't true. What you insinuated doesn't make any sense."

"I guess..." Looking down, Sarah's argument resonated in his head.

One thought jumped into Sarah's mind and she went over to the calendar on the wall. "Hey, if I remember it correctly they celebrate Mother's Day on a different date in the USA. Let me check on my phone."

They both waited in silent anticipation while Sarah googled on her phone.

"Aye, I was right. In the US, Mother's Day is celebrated each year on the second Sunday in May." Sarah showed George her findings on her phone.

George nodded.

"You see; Aileen should be back long before then so she won't be celebrating the American Mother's Day with Alistair either." Sarah was mightily pleased with her findings and logic, hoping to make her husband stop merging all those negative thoughts in his head.

George nodded again and this time it seemed he was agreeing with Sarah's words.

"Yes, life is unfair but you don't know about other people's lives and how they actually are unless they really share with you their pain and struggles. Besides, you can't take out your frustrations at the misfortunes of your life on others," Sarah voiced her opinion. She saw from George's facial expression that a thousand thoughts were running through his head.

Without her needing to spell it out, George knew that Sarah was referring to the lives of Andrew, Alistair and Michelle but other names also popped into George's mind.

"It's getting rather late. I'm getting ready for bed now. Are you coming, love?"

"Just give me a few moments," George pleaded. Her words felt like someone pouring cold water over his head. They'd awoken and unlocked something inside him.

"Don't stay up too late! You just got back from the hospital today." As she was about to leave the room, she clearly heard George's admission.

"Thanks for listening and for not judging me. I must be a nightmare to live with these days. I am sorry."

"Just these days!" joked Sarah pulling a face and looking at George over her shoulder.

They both burst out laughing.

"Oh, you silly sod. Don't forget to take your medication," reminded Sarah with care in her voice. She yawned and stretched her arms and her body shivered in a sudden cold.

"Sure."

"Don't sit here too long it's cold." She adjusted the thermostat. She and George had become very conscious about the recent increase in energy bills and would only turn up the heating when it was absolutely necessary. "Good night."

"Good night. I will be in shortly."

"Phew." While walking to the bathroom Sarah heaved a sigh. *It has been a long day, or a long eventful eight or nine days rather, to say the least. So much has happened.*

Sitting alone in the kitchen, George contemplated his conversation with Sarah. He was tired but inexplicably felt enlightened. It was the first time he had an inkling that in order to improve his relationships and interactions with others changes had to be made, by him. Not that he knew how at that moment but he felt that by recognising it was already the first big step. Before he went to bed the last thought that came to his mind was that judging others and being envious of them was tiring.

Chapter 14 – 2023

In the days leading to Fredrich's memorial service in Germany, George's mood fluctuated wildly. Understandably, he was upset that he was not able to attend but then an invitation for Kimberly came from Nadine's family. Sarah and George were extremely pleased about the gesture. Luckily, Kimberly was able to travel there to represent him and that made him feel like he was somewhat included.

Kimberley came to Edinburgh one night before her trip. Preparing for Kimberly's trip, Sarah was relieved that George was preoccupied with it all and that distracted him from feeling left out.

A small TV crew were travelling along with Kimberly to film the ending of the search. Out of respect, Fredrich's death was mentioned in the narrative while the funeral was kept private. The filming of the memorial service was also done unobtrusively to avoid disrupting the event or upsetting the family. The main focus was on Kimberly's heart-warming meeting and interactions with Nadine and her other relatives. Kimberly also video-called from Germany so that Nadine could properly introduce her family to George and Sarah. After the final filming was done, they were able to have direct contact with each other and Nadine and her parents were hoping to visit George and Sarah in the coming months.

On Sunday, the day after the memorial service, George was having a cup of tea in the kitchen feeling restless.

"George, can you double-check whether it's a blue box or red box tomorrow?" asked Sarah from the living room, admiring the flowers and condolence cards they'd received.

"Let's see. Um, what is today's date, 12th March! So tomorrow is 13th March." George checked the calendar in the kitchen and walked to the living room to report back to Sarah. "It will be the red recycling box tomorrow."

"Look at those beautiful flowers people have sent. Oh, and these are from Aileen and Alistair, so thoughtful of them to order from the US."

"Look at this one!" exclaimed George in irritation, holding one of the condolences cards.

"What is the matter? Didn't you read it before?" asked Sarah, not paying attention to George's reaction.

"Read this!" George insisted, waving the card.

"What is wrong now?" Sarah grabbed the card from George's hand and read it again and inspected the card to try to understand George's whining. "What is wrong with it?" Sarah was taken aback by the depth of his sudden anger.

"Why can't people say what it is? Why do people have to say crap like 'Sorry for the passing of your loved one', say it like it is. My brother died. He died!" George exclaimed, kicking up a fuss.

"Yes, Fredrich died but there are many ways that people express their condolences. That may be how they were brought up, or maybe it's for religious reasons. You can't take stuff like that to heart and be offended by it!"

"I just don't understand why people have to sugar-coat it," grumbled George.

"Look, I understand that you're upset about Fredrich's death and not being able to attend his funeral and the memorial service but don't let that twist everything into something sinister in your mind!" Sarah shook her head in exasperation while she left the room, not wanting to hear any more about it. She thought it was best to leave him alone to cool down.

Sarah was surprised about George's sudden outburst considering that recently, since their last serious talk, George had been mindful of his words and had controlled his temper. At the same time, Sarah also understood it was his way of working out his grief and frustration.

In the days that followed, George was busy getting himself ready and filming a segment to be included in the final production where he talked about his thoughts on the search and shared his recent health scare which had prevented him from travelling to Germany to meet Fredrich and then to attend the memorial service. After that, all the buzz quieted down and Sarah returned back to work. George was feeling bored and anxious. Despite that he got on well with the rehabilitation exercise programme that the hospital had organised for him, he was worried about seeing the GP to talk about his mental health, hoping his prescription of antidepressant tablets would not be ended.

"What on earth are you doing?" questioned Sarah when she came home from work one day and found that George had emptied all the items from the kitchen cupboards and drawers and scattered them everywhere, including in the living room.

"What does it look like I'm doing, cleaning! I thought you would be happy that I'm up and doing something," defended George, beaming as though it was his new-found purpose in life. He looked so proud of his initiative, like he'd won a trophy of some sort.

"Aye... but you shouldn't take things too far. You should follow the rehabilitation programme and do your daily exercise. Did you go out for a walk?"

"I got distracted," grumbled George, puzzling over why Sarah made a big deal out of nothing.

"George, what about going back to your volunteering work once a week? It will do you good to get out of the house and meet people."

"I... I guess," he said hesitantly.

That evening when Sarah took out the rubbish she phoned Kimberly to unload her concerns.

"Maybe I could persuade Dad to attend meditation classes or acupuncture?" Kimberly suggested.

"Well, you can suggest it, but there's a slim chance he will agree to any kind of alternative treatments," said Sarah without much optimism. "What time are you coming on Saturday?"

"We'll arrive in the afternoon. The kids have made you a card." Kimberly attempted to cheer her mother up.

Kimberly and her family came to visit George and Sarah and stayed over the Mother's Day weekend. They made a call to Aileen and George was in a perky mood. As far as he could remember, it was the first Mother's Day he hadn't celebrated with Aileen, so having his family around and being able to see and hear Aileen through the screen that day was particularly comforting to him.

A few weeks passed and George did take up Sarah's suggestion to go back to his volunteering work, once a week to start with and then extending to twice a week. He felt extremely pleased at the sense of being needed and that he was contributing to a good cause. Much to Sarah's delight, she started to notice a transformation in George, especially since he'd begun walking to the volunteer place and back, a thirty-minute journey each way.

One day, out of the blue, George received a call from Andrew asking how he was doing. Andrew and Kimberly followed each other on social media, which was where he'd learned about George's heart surgery. He'd wanted to call right away but was advised to wait till George's condition became more stable.

George was extremely happy at Andrew's call. It'd been on his mind to contact him, to somehow try to apologise, but was put off by his pride in combination with feeling embarrassed about his past interactions with him. George was worried that Andrew would not accept his call.

The two cousins agreed to meet up in Cramond a few days later to have a walk along the beach promenade.

The evening before they were to meet up, George was obviously apprehensive about it. He thought his surgery was a blessing in disguise that gave him the chance to reflect and see different perspectives about life in general and also his way of dealing with people in the past. He was nevertheless afraid that he might screw up again. He knew himself too well and realised that the only obstacle that would prevent and sabotage mending the relationship with Andrew was himself.

"Why are you checking your phone every five minutes?" queried Sarah, sensing her husband's anxiety from the way he wasn't paying attention to his favourite TV show after their evening tea.

"I... I'm just worried that Andrew might want to cancel," revealed George with his head down.

"Oh." The comment caught her off guard. "Don't overthink it. What about another cup of tea?" Sarah attempted to distract her husband from his needless worries.

He shook his head and was overwhelmed with an unexpected feeling of being suffocated. "I need a walk. I won't be long." Not waiting for Sarah's response, George leapt off the seat and walked out. "Phew!" He let out a breath once he closed the door behind him.

For a while he walked aimlessly, drifting around their local area tightly clutching his phone in his hand before eventually sitting down on a bench. He fiddled with his phone some more and then got bored with his constant checking and, without any particular intention, he pressed the photos button. Flipping through photos of his grandchildren put a smile on his face and eased the knot in his stomach. He then reached the photos from the trip to Orkney in 2021, less than two years ago, when he had first met Alistair and Michelle. The pictures suddenly brought to mind a strange incident that had happened during that trip.

He didn't recall whether it was the second or the third day of their bus tour that they visited the prehistoric stone circle at Brodgar. For some reason, he wasn't able to explain he'd been magnetically drawn to a particular stone and he had spontaneously closed his eyes and pressed his hand against it. At that moment he felt a warm energy moving through his body and mind which made him think tenderly of his father. '*What is going on? How long have I been doing this?*' George was frightened of this strange experience so he opened his eyes and wondered if anyone had seen him. He peeked around and saw that no one was paying any attention to him because everyone was busy walking around touching the magnificent circle of stones. He didn't share this incident with anyone, especially given that he had never believed in any kind of spiritual mumbo jumbo. He thought that perhaps his experience might have been triggered by the fact that his father had just died less than a year prior to the trip. Nevertheless, at that rare moment, he'd a vague appreciation of why his father had never let him be close to him. '*It must have been so hard for him that his wife*

committed suicide and then he had to raise me, the one
person that reminded him of her.'

"Evening, George," greeted a passing neighbour as he was carrying a rubbish bag in his hand towards the communal bin nearby.

George raised his head and acknowledged the man with a nod and then noticed he was waving with his phone in his hand. Both he and the neighbour grinned. George waited for the neighbour to go back to the building before he returned to his thoughts.

'Why am I thinking about that strange incident now?'

Suddenly it dawned on him that it was because it was related to his father and that he was seeing Andrew the day after. *'Wonder how pleased my father would be knowing that I have a second chance with Andrew? From what Mum has told me, I know that one of his regrets was not being able to patch things up with his brother.'*

George started to ponder how difficult it must have been for Andrew and his mum when his father abandoned them when he was just an infant. George was then overcome with guilt and a feeling of being selfish that he had pushed Andrew to take part in the TV programme without appreciating his cousin's tangled feelings. Now that he had started to think about things from Andrew's point of view, he wasn't able to stop. He reflected back on his own behaviour towards Andrew and how he had made a fool of himself on numerous occasions. He felt a red flush of embarrassment creep over his face. From Andrew, he then thought about Alistair and his own unfounded distrust towards him and his feeling of being inferior when he was around him. A realisation suddenly surfaced in George's mind. It must have been heart-breaking for Alistair growing up not being with his real mother and knowing that his mum had remarried and had another boy calling her mum as well. That evening as he sat alone on the bench, George came to feel a profound sense of appreciation for Andrew and Alistair's hardships and struggles in life.

As he rose from his seat and began walking home, he felt his posture relax somewhat and the load on his shoulders ease. He was realistically aware that he wouldn't be able to change overnight but being aware of his behaviour and acknowledging the causes would help him to break his patterns of feeling insecure and self-conscious.

'*Small steps, small steps.*' Looking up at the sky he encouraged himself and felt optimistic thinking about Andrew, Alistair and his German relatives that he was about to meet in the near future. With mixed feelings of enlightenment and perplexity about his realisation, George walked briskly towards his door as his bladder was urging him to use the bathroom.

Chapter 15 – 2023

"Hi, George. Wow, I hardly recognise you; you look younger and more upbeat!" praised Andrew. He approached and gave George a pat on his shoulder.

"Thanks. You look well too." George kept his answer short with his upper body stiff. He was without doubt self-conscious about what had happened during their last conversation less than a year ago where he'd foolishly lashed out at Andrew.

A silence fell on them as the two cousins walked along the promenade tilting their heads upwards and enjoying the early spring sunshine that mid-April day.

"Nice, isn't it," Andrew initiated the conversation while loosening his scarf and undoing the two top buttons of his jacket.

"Aye. Oh, we're lucky with the weather," replied George. "It was a cloudy morning, and I thought it might rain."

"So, how are you doing?"

"I'm better. I aim to go back to work in a few weeks' time. I'm following the rehabilitation programme, doing my exercise and eating healthier." George proudly pointed at his waist, which had evidently shrunk since their last meeting.

"Yes, I noticed that. Nice to see that you're better. You seem to have a lighter demeanour in general," praised Andrew.

"Thanks. Aye, lots have happened and changed since we last talked... I... I'm truly sorry about how our last conversation ended. It was wrong of me to impose on you to take part in the TV programme. It wasn't my place to pressure you. It was totally uncalled for on my part." George carefully chose the words to deliver his apology that he'd rehearsed multiple times in his head.

"I... nothing to apologise for. Though much appreciated. You meant well and I wish I had your courage."

"I'm glad that you phoned me. You're a bigger man than I am," stated George with a genuine look on his face, showing his sincere appreciation for Andrew's peace offering.

"Not at all. Oh, I'm lost for words to describe how sorry I am about the search. Um..." Andrew had become tongue-tied at first because he was taken back at George's straight-to-the-point talk of making amends. Also, he wasn't able to express the depth of his sorrow about Freya and Fredrich.

"Ah, thanks, and thanks for the flowers and the card you sent. I am pleased to know that Kimberly updated you about the progress of my search. You see, we're not allowed to post anything yet on social media or share anything in public until the episode is aired."

"When will that be?"

"I think sometime in autumn. It's now in the editing stage."

"Nice, I look forward to watching it. Should we sit down?" suggested Andrew, pointing at a bench nearby.

As they sat down, looking out at the sea, Andrew became very thoughtful and it was clear to George from the expression on his face that he was formulating how to voice what was on his mind.

"I still owe you an explanation for why in the end I decided not to go further with the search project. I..." Andrew paused for a while before he continued, "My father left us when I was just a toddler and I've no memories of him. I don't know if I can take it..."

"Take what?"

Andrew didn't answer but had a troubled expression on his face, with his eyebrows pulled downwards, his eyes squinting and his mouth clamped tightly shut.

"Is anything the matter?"

"Sorry, I was lost in my own thoughts," said Andrew. "What if he's dead? My father left us for whatever reason and made the decision not to keep in contact... So, what would happen when and if I found him and he had another family and didn't want anything to do with me? I don't want to be rejected all over again. Growing up I blamed myself, thinking I was the reason he left... Truth be told... in the back of my mind there is a small part of me that still thinks so. I already lost my mother and my son so I'm not going to take the risk of getting rejected by him again."

George was totally stunned that Andrew carried with him such profound pain and grief. When he thought about Andrew he seemed always to be so confident with such a successful career. One would never have guessed he would have such self-doubt.

The atmosphere became sombre. The two cousins sat next to each other, reflecting on their lives. After a while George broke the ice, putting a hand on Andrew's back.

"Listen, I'm very sorry to hear about your struggles. I fully understand why you would not want to get hurt again."

"Thanks…" said Andrew and with his throat tightened he took a moment to compose himself. He felt a sensation of warmth through his body with George's hand on his back, realising how great it was that they were actually getting to know each other as family members.

"I also have something I'd like to share with you," George told him cautiously. "If that's all right with you of course?"

"Sure."

"I have to admit that there has been something haunting me for a while as well."

"Take your time," comforted Andrew when he saw George start breathing unevenly, seemingly building himself up to something.

After a few moments, George calmed down. "At times I could feel my own head pounding from thinking about it. Both Sarah and Kimberly told me not to dwell on it and I understand they mean well, but… but, on the other hand, I'm still grasping, trying to find peace with it." George lowered his head slightly, looking downcast.

"About what? What's wrong?" asked Andrew with a hint of alarm, baffled at George's dramatic gesture and the awkward words tumbling from his mouth.

"Well..." George began but was unsure how to finish explaining what was on his mind. He paused for a moment again before continuing, "We think my mother committed suicide due to survivor's guilt. Erm, a new term I've learned. I can't help thinking... thinking... thinking that she chose death over being alive to raise me."

Andrew was stunned for a moment at George's bravery in sharing the core trigger that had apparently been mentally plaguing him.

"My goodness! But, you can't possibly think that! Your birth mother was not well, it must have been caused by the traumas she endured and all the inhuman and ungodly treatment she experienced and witnessed during the war. I can't even begin to imagine the pain she carried as a result of all that."

"I know. Ever since I was old enough I spent sleepless nights trying to figure out the despair she endured and what her last desperate thoughts were before she put the rope around her neck..." George stopped because his voice had unexpectedly cracked.

Andrew turned to face George and he could almost sense the tension in him.

"A..." Andrew felt a lump in his throat as well. He was so taken aback at George trusting him while being so vulnerable. It was the first time Andrew had seen this side of George, carrying the dreadful burden of losing his mother to suicide. As he now had a better understanding of George he became aware that all the earlier frictions between them were ultimately minor. Years of not knowing each other and the differences between them simply had generated a few misunderstandings and unrealistic expectations at first. "Are you all right?" asked Andrew once he had composed his own emotions.

George nodded, tight-lipped. He forced a smile but was betrayed by the wrinkles on his forehead as he subconsciously frowned.

"So sorry that you have been tormented by this... But one thing I'm certain of, she would be so happy knowing that you're now connected with the German side of the family!" reassured Andrew, his way of injecting something positive into a tragic past.

"I know... But what strained my mind the most was that she didn't have to die after all! If she had only known Fredrich was alive! But why couldn't she be alive for me? Did she think I was unworthy of love?" George's face crumpled when the last word came out of his mouth.

"Yes, I understand your frustration. What happened to her and you was not fair. It was such an unjust situation that led to her taking her own life."

"I know. I know that I need to let it go but it's easier said than done," confessed George, shrugging his shoulders.

"Have you heard anything more from your relatives in Germany?"

"Aye, Nadine, she's Fredrich's granddaughter, and some of her family members are coming to Edinburgh in the beginning of May, in time for Mother's Day in Germany. They want to pay their respects by visiting Freya's grave."

"That is such a meaningful occasion," Andrew responded with an upbeat tone.

"Also, I will be sixty later this year so they want to give me an early celebration as well."

"How wonderful! You don't look one day older than fifty-nine," Andrew joked to lighten the mood, knowing it was the sort of humour George would like.

"Thanks. Charming!"

They both laughed out loud.

"I've stopped drinking all carbonated drinks. I went cold turkey," announced George, proud of himself. He grabbed two bottles of mineral water from his backpack and handed one to Andrew.

"Ta." Andrew waited for George to continue because he didn't know how to respond to George's sudden statement.

"I want to be healthier and, to be fair, I'm not doing my health or my teeth any favours drinking them," explained George.

"Good for you."

"I heard this comedian's joke once. I don't remember exactly how he said it but it was something like he thinks it's laughable seeing fat people sipping diet Coke or Zero with straws as if *that* will help them become thinner! In their own fantasy world maybe.

273

They're just in denial. What they really need to do is stop drinking any of them and get out jogging!"

"Wow! Harsh," voiced Andrew in disagreement, raising his eyebrows.

"I know. He said that a comedian's job is to provoke."

"To provoke? I thought a comedian should be funny!"

"Well, from my own experience, it's quite true what he said because I used to be like that too, lying to myself and thinking I would not gain weight that way."

"Well, I'm impressed with your determination!"

"Aye, meeting my German relatives gives me the motivation to lose weight and get healthy. I'm really looking forward to getting to know them. There are still many puzzles that need to be solved. We'd gathered bits and pieces from Fredrich's adoption file, like that he was found in an old woman's home. The old woman's daughter worked as a guard in a concentration camp. After the war ended the guard was put on trial along with many of her colleagues and was eventually sent to prison to wait for her final sentence. She first said she'd found Fredrich abandoned but then changed her statement and confessed that she'd snatched Fredrich from a woman sent to the concentration camp." George paused to take a much-needed breath and exhaled.

"Unbelievable." Shaking his head with his eyes wide open Andrew gasped in amazement at what he was hearing.

"Listen, there is more," George continued. "Apparently, she refused to give any details about the child's mother. So, we still don't know her motive for changing her statement or how or why the authorities found Fredrich and came to the conclusion that he wasn't the guard's own child. The guard also said in her defence that she lost her husband, who was killed during the war, and she had longed for a child of her own. Seeing an opportunity, she took the child from a woman and gave it to her elderly mother, who was in ill health herself, to take care of."

"What an astonishing tale with so many twists. Do you know any more?" asked Andrew, waiting with bated breath.

"Well. The guard committed suicide in her jail cell so that was all we know from that end. Another peculiar thing was that we learnt from my mum what my old man told her, that my birth mother was separated from her husband by the Nazis and her baby was taken from her by a female guard. So, if it were the same guard, why would she spare sending my birth mother to the gas chamber? One would think it would have been the easiest approach to cover up her crime of stealing the baby?" asked George, not that he was expecting any answer from Andrew.

"Yes, I agree."

"My old man mentioned to my mum once that my birth mother had been told by the guard that her husband and her baby boy were both killed."

"How sad, and how devastating it must have been for her!" Andrew exclaimed with sadness in his voice. "If only Freya knew Fredrich was alive!"

"Hopefully, by the time we all meet up we'll be able to find out more. Aye. Nadine has submitted enquiries to the German authorities. From our side, we're also curious how my birth mother first went to London and then to Edinburgh. Kimberly is taking the lead to find out more. She submitted an enquiry to the Registrar's Office in Edinburgh," George explained enthusiastically.

"I really hope you can get to the bottom of it," said Andrew, full of encouragement.

"Aye. Cheers. Me too."

"Wait, what about Fredrich? Did he remember anything or say anything to his family?" With wide eyes, Andrew was eager for a reply.

"No. We asked the same question and were told that he was too young to remember but we believe it could be that he blocked out the trauma in his brain," responded George scratching his head.

"I see. I read once that some survivors of horrific trauma do unconsciously block out the event. Dissociating and detaching from the experience serves as a pain reliever."

"Yeah. Kimberly said something similar. I don't have any memories of my birth mother either." George agreed without any hesitation, shaking his leg and massaging it. His leg started to get numb because they'd been sitting there for a while.

"Oh…" Andrew mumbled. In fact, what he didn't share was his own experience of this subject, relating to him partially blocking out memories of receiving the news about his son's death. He shook his head and quickly realised he would rather talk about something else before the atmosphere became too sombre. "How are Kimberly and Sarah?"

"They're fine. They send their regards. Oh, they're encouraging me to research about the Holocaust."

"Must be very hard to learn about such a devastating part of history!"

"Aye, that's why I'm still not ready to do it myself. Not yet. I'm too afraid to face it," confessed George.

"Fully understandable."

"Hey, thanks for listening," said George as he patted Andrew's shoulder.

Andrew smiled and turned his head to look at George and was met by his appreciative grin. Something Mama Evelyn used to say popped into Andrew's head and warmed his heart, that not all issues or problems need to or can be solved. Some just need to be heard.

"By the way, I had a discussion with Sarah the other night and she asked me to list the three most horrific or memorable world events in our lifetime so far. I mean that had affected us. I—"

"What did you say?" interrupted Andrew, showing his curiosity.

"Well, I said what happened to Jews during the Second World War for one. And the second one would be 9/11 in the US and then the pandemic. What about you?"

"Oh, I need to have a think. I can't top anything you mentioned. Though one event that greatly affected me was Lady Diana's death. Of course, it can't be compared to the events you listed."

George nodded in agreement and they sat in companionable silence for a while.

For a moment Andrew felt a sudden fatigue overcome him. He shut his eyes and exhaled slowly, longing for a nap. He was overwhelmed by the story George had shared with him and their emotional exchanges. When he opened his eyes and turned his head he noticed George was obviously struggling to keep his own eyes open as well.

"Sleepy?" asked Andrew as he tapped gently on George's shoulder.

George opened his eyes and stretched his arms. "Aye. I haven't felt this relaxed for a long time."

Andrew smiled and picked up the conversation again. "Oh, before I forget, how is Aileen? She must be thrilled that you're advancing so much in your research."

"Yes, she is. Oh, she's coming back next week. She sends her regards as well. She was so happy when I told her that we arranged to meet up. She wants to invite you to her place for dinner one evening."

"Oh, that would be lovely! I would also like to meet Kimberly and her family one day."

"Yes, that could certainly be arranged. She's looking forward to meeting you too in fact."

"Can you imagine our fathers laughing somewhere up above and being pleased that we met up again?" wondered Andrew with a genuine smile.

"Aye, I can," avowed George, beaming from ear to ear before he turned his head to face the sea.

With their eyes closed, the two cousins sat silently bathed in the remaining sunlight and the sea breeze.

The conversation George had had with Andrew brought random thoughts to his head. First, he remembered not long ago someone advised him about the gift of finding compassion for others and most importantly for oneself. Then a surreal sensation of gratitude overcame him as he considered his recent heart surgery and that he'd found his German relatives. He started counting his blessings. Aileen had devoted her life to being a mother to him. Not to mention all the love and support he received from Sarah and the joy of having Kimberly and her family. He also thought about his past dealings with Andrew, Alistair and many others where he had put his foot in his mouth. His own insecurity played a huge part in crippling his opportunities in building relationships with others.

Chewing over his talk with Andrew that day, George now saw Andrew in a different light. He recognised that they both had unanswered questions and unresolved issues. They had both been wounded by their parents' choices and their families' difficult pasts which had moulded them to become who they were and that had influenced their outlook on life. However, they were in fact actually very similar, searching to be worthy and to feel loved. Another thing they had in common was they never handled rejection well. George was about to share his thoughts with Andrew but at the last moment, he grasped that no words were needed, at least for the moment, because he would like to believe that they had found an unspoken understanding of each other. It was with this thought in mind that George felt a hope ignite for a real friendship with Andrew in the future. He even dared imagine that if he could build bridges with his cousin then surely the other relationships in his life could be fostered as well. He relished the rare occasion of feeling optimistic and comfortable in his own skin.

As George had been sitting in the same position for a while, sweat was trickling down his back. He adjusted his posture and leaned forward a bit from the back of the bench to let the air circulate but then he felt a sudden chill. His eyes started twitching as well so he opened them. He went and grabbed a scarf from his backpack and as he did so something fell out from it and woke Andrew up.

"Oh, how long have I been dozing?"

"Not too long." George bent over to pick up a small transparent bag from the ground.

"What are those?" asked Andrew, kicking his legs out.

"I meant to show you photos of my birth mother and Fredrich." George carefully took out the photos from the bag and handed them to Andrew.

"Thanks." As Andrew looked through them with great interest he also noticed other items remaining in the bag. "And those?"

"They're postcards of Vincent van Gogh's paintings. We found them along with the photos. We believe they belonged to my birth mother but we're not certain."

"Intriguing. I visited the Museum of Modern Art in New York last year and saw it displayed there." Andrew pointed at one picture. "This one is called *The Starry Night*. Just happens to be my favourite painting of his. Did you know there is a song dedicated to his life…"